THE SILVER HORSESHOE

John Arbinger receives an anonymous note — offering 'protection' from criminal gangs in exchange for £5,000 — with the impression of a tiny silver horseshoe in the bottom right-hand corner. Ignoring the author's warning about going to the police, Arbinger seeks the help of Superintendent Budd of Scotland Yard. But Budd is too late to save Arbinger from the deadly consequences of his actions, and soon the activities of the Silver Horseshoe threaten the public at large — as well as the lives of Budd and his stalwart companions . . .

GERALD VERNER

THE SILVER HORSESHOE

Complete and Unabridged

LINFORD
Leicester

First published in Great Britain

First Linford Edition
published 2015

A catalogue record for this book is available
from the British Library.

ISBN 978–1–4448–2557–2

Published by
F. A. Thorpe (Publishing)
Anstey, Leicestershire

Set by Words & Graphics Ltd.
Anstey, Leicestershire
Printed and bound in Great Britain by
T. J. International Ltd., Padstow, Cornwall

This book is printed on acid-free paper

To the Paternosters

1

The Beginning of the Terror

The first hint of the menace came in the form of a letter to the pleasant breakfast table of John Arbinger, one fine spring morning. It was a duplicated blank, certain portions of which had been filled in with pen and ink, and it brought a frown to the genial face of the bookmaker as he read it:

> 'There are certain isolated gangs in this country who are acquiring large incomes by the intimidation of book-makers. We guarantee you immunity from their depredations and protection from physical violence in exchange for the sum of five thousand pounds, which represents a year's subscription to our society. This money, in notes of one-pound denomination, should be ready for our messenger who will

call for it at midnight on May 10th. You are advised in your own interests to comply with this request, since failure to do so will inevitably result in your death. Any attempt to communicate with the police will be treated as a breach of faith and punished accordingly.'

It was unsigned, but stamped in the lower right-hand corner was the impression of a tiny horseshoe in silver.

Mr. Arbinger sniffed contemptuously as he tossed the letter across the table. 'What do these people take me for — a mug?'

His daughter opposite him looked up from reading her newspaper.

'Read it!' he growled, helping himself liberally to marmalade.

Marjorie Arbinger picked up the letter and studied it, frowning. A slim, straight-backed girl of twenty-two, her golden head rivalled the glory of the daffodils that graced the table.

'What are you going to do about this?' she asked seriously.

2

'Nothing! I've been threatened before but I'm still alive. If these people think they're going to scare five thousand pounds out of me by that kind of balderdash they'll find they've tackled the wrong man.'

'But you're going to do something, surely?' she insisted. 'May 10th — that's Saturday.'

'Right! And if their precious messenger turns up he'll get more than he bargains for,' he prophesied grimly. 'Don't worry yourself, Marjorie. It's just a try-on.'

'I wish you'd do something about it, all the same,' she said with a worried frown. 'It sounds too cold-blooded to be treated lightly.'

He gulped down the remainder of his coffee and leaned back in his chair, smiling. 'It's just a new form of the old race-gang racket!' he declared contemptuously. He got up and patted her shoulder. 'Don't you worry yourself,' he said, taking the letter gently from her fingers. 'I'll call into Scotland Yard on my way to the office and they'll soon deal with this nonsense.'

'But they warn you against going to the police,' she muttered doubtfully.

'Of course they do!' Arbinger chuckled. 'But what they want and what they're going to get are two different matters. Forget all about it, darling. I was a fool to have shown it to you.'

'But you will be careful?' she urged.

'It's not I who will have to be careful,' he laughed. 'It's the people who wrote this letter.' He glanced at his watch. 'I must go now, Marjorie. I'll probably be late tonight. I've got a business dinner engagement.' He kissed her lightly and went out into the hall, where his butler was waiting to help him on with his overcoat.

During his journey to town he was more occupied with the appointment he had mentioned than with the menacing letter. Nevertheless, when the car reached the Chelsea Embankment, he pressed the button of the microphone at his side and ordered his chauffeur to stop at the entrance to Scotland Yard. He got out, and entering that forbidding building put an inquiry to the man on the door.

He was shown into a cheerless waiting room, and after a short delay conducted up several flights of stone stairs to an equally cheerless office in which sat, behind a broad desk, one of the largest men he had ever seen. The man's sleepy eyes regarded Mr. Arbinger from a face that was in keeping with the rest of his appearance.

'Sit down, sir,' he said huskily, his voice rumbling up from the vast depths of his capacious stomach. 'I understand you've got an inquiry concernin' a threatenin' letter?'

'Yes.' The bookmaker pulled the only vacant chair in the room up to the other side of the desk, sat down, and plunged his hand into his breast pocket. 'Here's the thing. It came by this morning's post.'

Taking the letter, Mr. Budd hoisted himself into a more convenient position and examined the envelope.

'Posted in the West Central district in time to catch the last delivery,' he murmured slowly. 'H'm!' Very delicately he withdrew the single sheet of paper and studied it. 'How many people have handled this?'

'Only myself and my daughter. And, of course, the person who wrote it.'

'It wasn't written, it was duplicated,' Mr. Budd said. 'Your name, the amount, an' the date have been filled in after in ink. It looks as if you're not the only person who may be receiving one of these things. No signature, just a little horse-shoe in silver. Interestin' and peculiar.' He suppressed a yawn, and the bookmaker thought he looked rather bored. 'I'll bet that the man who sent this was wearin' gloves when he put it in the envelope.' He drew a pad towards him. 'Now, sir, if you wouldn't mind answerin' a few questions . . .'

They seemed to Arbinger to be mostly irrelevant, but he answered to the best of his ability.

'I think that's all, sir,' said Mr. Budd at length. 'Leave this to us, and don't worry. We'll attend to everythin'.' He pressed a bell-push, opened a drawer, and taking out a large envelope enclosed the letter in it.

A messenger came in answer to Mr. Budd's summons and the big man handed him the envelope. 'Take that along to the F.P. department,' he said, 'and ask 'em to let me have a report as soon as possible. I don't suppose there'll be any results,' he added pessimistically, when the man had gone. 'Our best plan'll be to set a trap for this messenger feller when he calls for the money on Saturday.'

'You think he'll come?' asked Arbinger sceptically.

The stout superintendent nodded. 'These horseshoe people are hopin' to frighten you out of five thousand pounds, and there'd be no sense in not sendin' someone to collect it. My advice to you, sir, is to say nothin' about this letter to anyone. I'll arrange to have a close watch kept on your house on Saturday, and any stranger who puts in an appearance'll get a warm welcome.'

Arbinger rose, extending his hand. 'It's very kind of you, Superintendent. I'll leave it to you then.'

The bookmaker took his leave, and he had barely gone when the lugubrious

7

Sergeant Leek slouched in.

'Who was that feller?' he asked.

'That,' said Mr. Budd, carefully piercing the end of one of his black cigars which he had taken from his waistcoat pocket, 'was Mr. John Arbinger, the well-known turf commission agent.'

'A bookie, eh?' said Leek. 'What was he doin' here?'

'He heard you was interested in racin',' said the big man, 'and called to see if you'd like to open an account.'

'How did he get my name?' asked the astonished Leek.

Mr. Budd sighed wearily. 'Haven't you got *any* sense of humour?'

'I don't see anythin' funny,' protested Leek.

'You wouldn't,' broke in his superior, 'not even if you looked in a mirror. Arbinger came because he's had a threatenin' letter.'

He explained, and had just finished when there came a tap on the door and a messenger appeared with a report from the Fingerprint Department. The test had revealed two sets of prints and a smudged impression of a thumb in the top left-hand corner.

'The thumbprint's mine,' said Mr. Budd, 'and the other two are probably Arbinger's and his daughter's. We can check up on that.' He blew a cloud of evil-smelling smoke towards the dingy ceiling and frowned. 'I wonder if there's an American back of this?' he murmured.

He picked up the house telephone and asked to be put through to the Aliens Department. 'Hello!' he said when the connection was made. 'This is Superintendent Budd speakin'. You might check up on all the American crooks who've landed in this country within the last few months . . . I want their names and addresses and anythin' that's known about 'em . . . Yes, let me know as soon as you can, will you?'

He dropped the instrument back on its rack and hunched himself lazily in his chair.

'That's all we can do at the moment,' he murmured, closing his eyes. 'I wonder if anyone else has had one of them demands?'

'Maybe it's a bluff,' suggested Leek, 'or somebody playin' a joke on this feller.'

'They wouldn't have had it duplicated,' said the superintendent. 'No, I don't think it's a joke or a bluff, but we shall know on Saturday.'

He was to know before that date, and the knowledge was to give him a profound shock.

* * *

John Arbinger spent an uneventful day. His morning was occupied with his usual business, and he lunched, as was his habit, at the Sporting Club. He was curious to learn if any of his confreres had received a similar letter, but apparently none of them had; or if they had, they made no mention of the fact.

In the evening he changed at his office and went to keep his dinner appointment with Lord Sevenways. In the interest of the ensuing business discussion he completely forgot the Silver Horseshoe letter and the threat which it contained.

He was driven home at half-past ten, a

happy and contented man, reaching the big house on the outskirts of Putney Heath just after eleven. His daughter had gone to bed, but Ronson, his dignified butler, was waiting up for him. As he helped him off with his coat, he said, 'I've put sandwiches and whisky in the study, sir.'

'All right, Ronson,' Arbinger said with a nod. 'I shan't require anything more.'

Those words, the last he was ever to utter, were singularly appropriate.

The butler wished him good night and as he turned to go to his pantry, heard him enter the study and close the door.

The scream and the crash of breaking glass that followed coincided with a curious noise 'like a badly silenced motorcycle', as he described it after. Thinking his master had had an accident, the alarmed servant hurried to the door of the room, turned the handle and entered. He stood on the threshold staring in horror at what he saw.

There was not a pane of glass left intact in the long French windows that opened into the garden. The polished top of the

11

desk that stood near them was scored and splintered, and a bowl of spring flowers was smashed to fragments.

On the floor lay John Arbinger in a pool of blood welling from the three bullet holes in his once-immaculate shirt front.

⋆   ⋆   ⋆

Mr. Budd was in bed sleeping peacefully when the urgent call came through, but in spite of this handicap he was on the scene of the tragedy within two hours of the first alarm being given. The divisional inspector and his men had already made a preliminary investigation when he arrived, but nothing had been disturbed.

It was the first machine-gun killing that the stout superintendent had ever seen; and after looking at what remained of the pleasant-faced, genial man who had sat in his office that morning, he had no wish to repeat the experience.

'They must have sprayed the room with shots, sir,' said the grizzled inspector, his tanned face rather pale. 'Look at the top of the desk — smashed to bits!'

'They meant to make sure,' grunted Mr. Budd, eyeing the damage sleepily. 'Has the doctor seen him?'

'Yes,' the inspector answered. 'He's with the daughter now. She took it badly, poor girl.'

'I'm not surprised.' The big man's face was stern as he looked down at the sprawling figure on the stained carpet. 'Submachine guns are nasty things, Bennet.'

'I suppose he got on the wrong side of one of these race-gangs,' Bennet remarked, shaking his head. 'Though they don't usually go further than a beating up — '

'This was no ordinary race gang,' broke in Mr. Budd. 'This is somethin' new, and I don't like it, Bennet.'

The murder of Arbinger had shocked him and filled him with a curious sense of responsibility. When the bookmaker had brought him the letter that morning he had never expected anything like this to happen, and he felt as though he was personally to blame. During his long experience he had seen many anonymous communications, but the threats contained in them were seldom carried out, and he had been inclined to treat the 'horseshoe' letter more or less sceptically.

The people behind it, however, were evidently different to the usual run of such law-breakers. They had struck swiftly and ruthlessly, offering John Arbinger as an awful example to those who, in the future, might be tempted to ignore their demands. For the stout man was under no delusions concerning the real reason behind this crime. The bookmaker had not been killed merely because he had defied the warning and gone to the police; he had been killed because his death was likely to prove a great asset in the campaign that was to come. This was the beginning, Mr. Budd felt convinced. The letter to Arbinger had been a feeler. There would be others; and the people who received them, remembering the fate that had overtaken the bookmaker, would pay up readily. That was the real motive. When the murder became known it would be a brave man indeed who would risk sharing poor John Arbinger's fate.

He looked up as the door opened and a

thin grey-haired man came into the room. 'I've put Miss Arbinger to bed with a sedative,' said the newcomer, and Mr. Budd guessed that this was the divisional surgeon. His guess was confirmed when inspector Bennet introduced them.

'You've made your examination, I understand, Doctor,' said Mr. Budd, and the other nodded.

'Yes,' he said. 'Three bullets went through the chest and one through the shoulder. It was a quick death, that's one thing. He could scarcely have known what killed him.'

'They were waitin' outside the windows,' Mr. Budd murmured, 'and when he put on the light they opened fire. They couldn't have missed him.'

'It's a horrible thing to have happened!' snapped the doctor. 'A brutal way of killing a man.'

'I don't suppose they bothered about that,' said the superintendent. He turned to Bennet. 'You've had a look outside, I suppose?'

'Yes.' Bennet nodded. 'There are traces of two men having waited outside the

15

window. The ground's soft and their footprints were easily distinguishable. I've had them covered over so that you can see them.'

'I'll see the butler first,' said Mr. Budd. 'What's his name — Johnson?'

'Ronson,' corrected the inspector.

'Ah yes, Ronson. Let's have him in.'

Bennet rang the bell, and after a slight delay the white-faced butler answered the summons, clutching desperately at the last remnants of his dignity.

'Now, Ronson,' said Mr. Budd kindly, 'you've had a bad shock, so I'm not goin' to worry you more than I can help.'

'Thank you, sir,' said the portly man, keeping his eyes averted from the thing by the desk.

'But you were the first to make the discovery, and I'd like you to tell me just what happened,' continued Mr. Budd.

Ronson licked his lips and rather disjointedly explained.

'You heard nothin' before Mr. Arbinger came home?' asked the superintendent.

'Nothing at all!' declared the butler.

'Miss Arbinger had gone to bed, hadn't

she?' said the big man.

'Yes. She went to bed at half-past ten. We — we didn't expect the master home until late. She wasn't asleep, though. She'd been reading, and when she heard the scream and the breaking glass she came running down. I tried to prevent her seeing what had happened.'

'Pity you weren't successful,' broke in the doctor. 'It gave her a bad shock, and it'll be some time before she recovers.'

The muffled but insistent ringing of a bell coincided with the end of his sentence.

'That's the doorbell, sir,' said Ronson, looking from one to the other. 'Shall I answer it?'

'Yes, but don't admit anyone,' Mr. Budd said. 'Find out who it is and let me know.'

Ronson departed and the superintendent turned to his subordinate. 'Did you find out how these two men succeeded in getting into the grounds?' he asked.

'Over the wall at the end of the garden,' answered Bennet promptly. 'It runs along by the side of the heath, and there's a mark where it has been climbed. They came in a car. The constable on patrol saw it but didn't think there was anything wrong.'

'Constables never do,' murmured Mr. Budd. 'Can this feller give a description of the car?'

'Yes,' said the inspector. 'It was an old-fashioned Morris saloon. Unfortunately he didn't take the number.'

'He wouldn't!' grunted Mr. Budd. 'He'd know it was an old-fashioned Morris, of which there are thousands, but he wouldn't know the most important thing. Still, I suppose you can't blame him — ' He broke off as the constable who had been waiting in the hall thrust in his head.

'There's a feller here wants to see you, sir,' he announced. 'A man called Ashton from the *Morning Mail*.'

Mr. Budd clicked his teeth impatiently. 'Tell him to go away,' he growled irritably. 'I don't want to see any reporters!'

'Now, don't be difficult,' said a cheery voice, and the constable was pushed aside to reveal a freckled face belonging to a

18

young man in a soiled and disreputable macintosh. 'You don't know how important I am, Budd.'

Mr. Budd eyed the newcomer darkly. 'You'll know just how important you are,' he snarled, 'when you find yourself thrown out of here, Ashton. What d'you mean by forcing your way in like this?'

'You won't throw me out,' Ashton said calmly. 'I've got important information.'

'I've heard that one before,' growled the superintendent. 'I don't want you here. Is that plain enough?'

'As plain as your face!' retorted the reporter. 'Seriously, though, Budd,' he added earnestly, 'you'll be making a mistake if you send me away.'

'All right, I'll see you in the hall for two minutes,' Mr. Budd said ungraciously, 'and if you're tryin' to put one over on me you'll go out quicker'n you came in!' He pushed the reporter out of the room and followed, shutting the door behind him.

'Now,' he demanded, 'what's this precious information you've got?'

'Arbinger's dead, isn't he?' asked Peter curiously.

'Never mind who's dead,' snarled Mr. Budd. 'I'm not givin' *you* information; you're supposed to be givin' it to me.'

The other shrugged, dived his hand into the pocket of his shabby raincoat, and produced a crumpled envelope. 'Well, take a look at that,' he said, holding it out.

The stout man seized it suspiciously, saw that it was addressed to 'The News Editor of the *Morning Mail*, Bouverie Street, E.C.4.', and extracted the two sheets of paper it contained. One was a duplicate of the letter which the unfortunate John Arbinger had received that morning. The other was typewritten and ran:

* * *

'*The Society of the Silver Horseshoe begs to inform the* Morning Mail *that a copy of the enclosed demand was sent to Mr. John Arbinger at his house at Putney this morning. Mr. Arbinger foolishly ignored*

20

the *warning contained in the last paragraph and communicated with Scotland Yard.*

'Mr. Arbinger *has suffered the penalty which such breach of faith demands. R.I.P.*'

In the lower right-hand corner was the stamped impression of a horseshoe in silver.

'It came by hand half an hour ago,' said Peter. 'The night editor thought it was a hoax, but when we tried to phone and couldn't get any reply he sent me along. Is it true? Is Arbinger dead?'

The stout superintendent hesitated, then: 'Yes, he's dead,' he answered soberly. 'He was dead before this letter was delivered to your office.'

2

Lord Sevenways Is Worried

There were lights in odd rooms at Scotland Yard which burned throughout that night, testifying to the diligence of the weary men who had been hastily called from their beds to deal with the inquiry into the murder of John Arbinger. Records of known criminals whose histories associated them with similar crimes of violence were patiently examined, and from the information room went countless messages to district police stations asking that these men's whereabouts should be checked and their movements on the previous evening accounted for.

The cars of the mobile squad sped hither and thither at the behest of the radio operator, stopping in mean streets while the startled occupant of a house was disturbed from his slumbers and closely questioned. Men on bicycles went swiftly to the beats of patrolling con- stables carrying the still-wet news sheets with an account of the murder hot from the printing press at headquarters. A description of the car that had been seen in the vicinity of Arbinger's house was circulated throughout the country; and petrol stations, garage proprietors and men on point duty warned to detain it.

Mr. Budd, a tired and despondent man, sat in his cheerless office receiving the meagre reports as they came in and issuing further instructions, in a mood that was entirely pessimistic. The people who worked under the symbol of the Silver Horseshoe were something new in his experience, and even in this early stage he realised that he was up against a formidable task.

There were signs of unusually careful planning and a directing intelligence. The sending of the letter notifying Arbinger's death to the *Morning Mail,* together with a copy of the letter that had preceded it, had been a clever move. It ensured widespread publicity from which they would reap their harvest in the fear that would be planted in the breasts of other men when more of the demand letters went out. This had been Peter Ashton's view also, and Mr. Budd knew the reporter's reputation too well not to treat his ideas with respect.

'Their whole object is to create a panic,' declared Peter, when they had discussed the matter at the house at Putney. 'This Arbinger business is only in the nature of a preliminary skirmish. If you could see into the mind of the person behind these horseshoe letters, I believe you'd find he hoped and expected Arbinger to act as he did. He wanted the bookmaker to go to Scotland Yard so as to provide an excuse for killing him. This racket's been worked in America and it doesn't start operating until somebody's dead. That's the whole psychology behind it. The next man who gets one of those letters will probably pay up sooner than risk going the same way as Arbinger. And that's the state of mind these people are trying to create.'

The stout superintendent knew he was right. He also saw the danger that would result. The police would receive no notification when a 'horseshoe letter' had reached the intended victim, for he would be too scared to publish the fact.

He left the Yard as the yellow sunlight was flooding the streets, and went home to his little house at Streatham, a man greatly troubled in his mind.

The morning editions of the *Mail* contained no reference either to the tragedy or to the two letters, for the announcement from the Silver Horseshoe arrived too late for inclusion. The *Morning Mail's* companion paper, however, the *Evening Comet,* carried a full account of both the murder and the circumstances which had led to it. On the front page the two letters had been printed side by side.

The paper was brought to Lord Sevenways with his tea, and when he saw the headlines his thin face went pale and he uttered an exclamation.

'I beg your pardon, m'lord?' inquired the footman respectfully.

'Nothing, Jones! Nothing!' said his master.

The man bowed and withdrew, and Sevenways rapidly scanned the lurid account, the hand that held the newspaper shaking visibly. He was a man of forty-five who looked sixty. His pale straw-coloured hair was brushed to conceal the incipient baldness; his thin, lined face was petulant; the weak mouth, with its smear of moustache, tremulous.

He read the account twice, flung the newspaper on the floor, and rising to his feet began to pace the long book-lined room with nervous strides. The death of John Arbinger was a catastrophe that left him momentarily stunned. He paused by the window, looking out unseeingly into Lowndes Square.

He was still standing there when his wife came in. Lady Sevenways was fifteen years younger than her husband and still retained the startling beauty which had drawn countless admirers to the stalls when she had graced the Ziegfeld Follies. Tall, slim, with dark hair that accentuated the whiteness of her skin, Sybilla Horton had been the most photographed girl in New York, and her picture still appeared frequently in weekly magazines.

Her marriage to the insignificant Lord Sevenways had created something of a sensation in America, for she had met and married him within a month. There were unkind people who said the title must have been the attraction; that the prospect of becoming Lady Sevenways and a member of one of the oldest families in England had dazzled her. Nobody had suggested that she had married him for his money, for the impecunious state of the Sevenways' finances was common property. It never occurred to anyone that she might have married him because she was in love with him, and yet this was the bare truth.

He looked round as he heard her come in and at sight of his face she came forward quickly, concern in her big violet-blue eyes. 'What's the matter, Nicky?' she asked anxiously, in a voice that still retained an American burr. 'You look ghastly!'

'I've had rather a shock, m'dear,' he muttered. 'That fellow Arbinger, the man I dined with last night — he's been murdered!'

'Murdered? But — '

'Yes, murdered! A horrible thing! Shot to pieces with machine guns, in his study. I can scarcely believe it.' He licked his lips and she saw that he was trembling.

'Sit down and have some tea,' she said, and busied herself at the tray which up to now he had neglected. Her calm voice and manner did something to mitigate the shock to his nerves.

'It's ghastly — this sort of thing happening in England,' he said, taking his handkerchief from his pocket and wiping his face. 'Must have happened almost immediately after he left me.'

She handed him a cup of tea and he took it mechanically. 'Why are you so upset?' she asked curiously, after a pause. 'Was this man — what did you say his name was? — a particular friend of yours?'

'Arbinger. No.' He stirred the tea erratically so that it splashed over into the saucer. 'No — just a business acquaintance, but a good fellow. I betted with him occasionally.'

'The bookmaker?' She looked across at him in faint surprise, and he nodded.

'Yes — but a gentleman.' He was recovering from the first shock of the unexpected news. 'Eton and Oxford. It's . . . it's dreadful.' He sipped at the hot tea and set down the cup and saucer. 'It may mean that — that I shall have to let Broad Acres go.'

'Broad Acres?' Her eyes were wide. 'Why? What difference does this man's death make to Broad Acres?'

'He — Arbinger — was going to help me,' he muttered. 'The interest on the mortgage falls due next month and he was going to lend me the money.' He was not looking at her as he spoke, or he would have seen the queer expression that came into her eyes.

'You never told me,' she said softly.

'No; I hate worrying you over money matters, my dear,' he replied.

'But you should have told me,' she said reproachfully. 'Had you arranged this with — Mr. Arbinger?'

'Yes.' He took a cigarette from a box on the table and lit it clumsily. 'We fixed it up over dinner last night. He was sending me the cheque at the end of the week. Now I — I suppose I shall have to make other arrangements.'

'Well, don't worry too much, darling.' She got up and crossed over and perched herself on the arm of his chair. 'How much is this interest?'

'Six thousand pounds. About five times as much as I've got in the world!'

She was silent. She knew the struggle he had to make ends meet — had known it when she had married him, for he had been very frank concerning his financial position. The Berkshire estate brought in just enough to live on with care, but left no appreciable margin, certainly not sufficient to pay the interest on the heavy mortgage which his father had raised on the property to pay his betting losses.

'Perhaps something will turn up,' she said cheerfully. 'I've got an uncle somewhere in Australia — I've told you about him before. I believe he's worth

30

millions of dollars, and when he dies it all comes to me.'

He smiled and his thin, rather weak face was transformed. 'That sort of thing only happens in books, honey.' He clasped her fingers affectionately. 'And anyway, it would be your money.'

'Don't be silly!' she broke in quickly. 'It would be *our* money. I guess I'm as fond of Broad Acres as you are.' She kissed him lightly, and slipping from the chair arm stood up, patting her hair. 'You almost made me forget what I came to tell you,' she said. 'Vera Ellis rang up to ask me if I'd have a drink and a sandwich with her and go on to the new film at the Pavilion.'

'Are you going?' he asked.

'I thought I would,' she replied. 'We're not doing anything tonight, are we?'

'No, my dear. You run along,' he said indulgently. 'It'll do you good.'

She blew him a kiss and went over to the door. 'I shan't be late,' she said as she went out, but her face altered as she ascended the stairs to her room, and retained its thoughtful expression while

31

she changed her clothes. What would her husband say if he knew? she wondered. For Vera Ellis was not even in London and she had no intention of going within a mile of the Pavilion, to see a film which she had already seen.

* * *

To half a dozen different breakfast tables on the Saturday morning following the killing of John Arbinger came an equal number of letters bearing the symbol of the silver horseshoe. They were identically worded, except for the names and the amounts demanded, and the six recipients read them in varying degrees of panic compatible with their different temperaments. Five, after the lesson of the Putney tragedy, decided to follow the instructions meticulously and pay, however painful the process of parting with the money might be.

But the sixth was made of sterner stuff.

Mr. Jacob Bellamy was a bachelor and lived in an unpretentious house on the outskirts of Wimbledon, a pleasant little place with a large garden in which he spent most of his leisure hours. He had been a boxer before he had adopted the more lucrative profession of bookmaker, and in spite of the fact that he had run to fat, his muscles were still hard. He was capable of giving a very good account of himself, as certain of the 'boys' who had attempted little pleasantries now and again had discovered to their cost. The big burly figure, with its ugly face, was a familiar one on all the racecourses in the country, and although Bellamy's Limited was not quite in such a large way of business as some of its confreres, it was noted for its integrity and straight dealing.

He read the letter without any change of expression on his wooden face, put it carefully away in his wallet, and went on eating his breakfast. On his way up to his office he thought over the demand which had reached him, and decided upon the policy he would adopt. He had no intention of being blackmailed out of the three thousand pounds asked, but the idea of going to the police never entered his head. Here was a chance for some excitement, and he would handle the matter himself in conjunction with certain friends whose outlook on life was similar to his own.

Peter Ashton was lounging in the reporter's room at the *Morning Mail* offices when the telephone message came through.

'That you, boy?' inquired a familiar, husky voice. 'Bellamy speakin'. Listen, cock, I've got somethin' I want to tell you. Pop out and have a bite of lunch with me at one, will you?'

'Sure, Jacob,' said Peter. 'Where shall I meet you, at the club?'

'No,' answered Mr. Bellamy. He mentioned the name of a hotel in Fleet Street. 'Meet me in the bar there.'

'OK,' agreed the reporter, and went back to his chair thoughtfully. In the past he had been indebted to Jacob Bellamy for many a good story, for the bookmaker was friendly with all sorts and conditions of people, and items of news came his way that were usually interesting.

His musings were interrupted by the

appearance of a head thrust in the doorway. 'Ashton, the old man wants you,' said a voice curtly, and Peter rose to interview the news editor.

Mr. Sorbet looked up from his littered desk as the reporter entered, with a scowl on his lined face. It gave him a particularly ferocious appearance, though actually he was one of the mildest of men. 'Here, Peter,' he said, 'I've just been looking through this interview of yours with John Arbinger's daughter. It's muck!' He stabbed at the offending copy with a stubby blue pencil.

'I know it is,' agreed Peter coolly, with a grin, 'but it was the best I could do.'

He had not relished the task that had been assigned to him at all, and could still see the pale, grief-stricken face of the girl as it had looked at him when he had, reluctantly, to force himself upon her privacy.

'It'll do as a 'fill-up',' grunted the news editor, 'but can't you get something with more meat in it? The most sensational crime for months and we've got nothing to follow it up.'

'Have patience!' retorted Peter, who was privileged. 'You'll get enough excitement to satisfy even your depraved taste before long.'

Mr. Sorbet brightened. 'You think we shall hear more of this silver horseshoe stuff?'

'I'm certain of it!' declared Peter. 'That letter they sent out with the other, notifying Arbinger's death, was duplicated, and they wouldn't have gone to that trouble unless they'd intended sending out more.'

'No, but that doesn't mean we're going to hear about 'em,' grunted Mr. Sorbet. 'Not after what happened to Arbinger.'

'They won't *all* pay up and look pleasant,' said Peter, and remembered the telephone message from Bellamy.

Curiously enough he had not associated it with the silver horseshoe, but now he did, and he mentioned it to Sorbet.

'Bellamy, eh?' The news editor grimaced. 'They've got hold of a tough nut if they've started on him. Something'll blow up, and I don't mind betting it won't be Bellamy.' He knew the old ex-boxer had, in the early days when he was a reporter, attended many of the fights in which Jacob had prominently figured. 'Bellamy!' he repeated under his breath. 'I wonder if that's what he wants to see you about?'

'I don't know,' said Peter, 'but it seems possible. These people are specialising in bookies, and Bellamy's a bookie.'

'Well, go along and see him,' said Mr. Sorbet. 'And remember you're a reporter first and foremost, and we want a sensation.' He settled down to his papers, and Peter realised the interview was over.

It was one o'clock precisely when he turned into the entrance of the hotel in Fleet Street where the old man had arranged to meet him, and making his way to the bar he found Bellamy with a large cigar in the corner of his mouth and a double whisky in front of him.

'Hello, cock!' greeted the bookmaker. 'What you goin' to have?'

Peter chose a modest bitter.

'I've fixed a table,' said Jacob, 'in a quiet corner where we can talk.'

'What's in the wind?' asked the

reporter curiously.

'I'll tell you while we have grub, boy,' replied Bellamy. 'Cheerio!' He gulped down his whisky and replaced the cigar in his mouth. 'I've got something that'll interest you, but you've got to promise not to publish it in that rag of yours till I give the word, see? You and me are goin' to make the sparks fly!'

Peter promised, and finishing his beer, they went upstairs to the restaurant. When they were seated at the reserved corner table and the bookmaker had given the order for their lunch, Peter leaned forward. 'Now, what's this sensational news you've got?'

Old Jacob looked quickly round him, and then thrusting a huge head across the table he said in a low voice, 'I've had one of them letters. You know, same as what poor Arbinger 'ad.'

Peter was interested. 'When did you get it?'

'This mornin'. I've got it on me.' Bellamy took a gold-bound wallet from his breast pocket and extracted a folded paper. 'Don't let anybody see it,' he said

38

cautiously, pushing it towards his companion.

Peter nodded and unfolded the sheet. It was an exact replica of the one he had seen before, except that the amount in this case was three thousand pounds and the date May 12th. 'They're not giving you much time,' he remarked.

'I know,' said Bellamy. 'And the sooner the better, so far as I'm concerned.' He took back the demand and replaced it in his wallet, returning that also to his pocket.

'Are you going to notify the police?'

Mr. Bellamy shook his massive head. 'No bloomin' fear! What d'you take me for? I'm gonna deal with this on me own, or rather you and me and a couple of pals'll deal with it together.'

He waited while the waitress placed before him an enormous steak and brought vegetables and fish for Peter, and then, when she had gone, continued. 'This is my idea, an' it's what poor Arbinger ought to 'ave done in the first place. Listen, cock! I'm goin' to pretend to fall in with these people's demands, wait for their blinkin' messenger to arrive at midnight on Monday, give 'im the doings, and let you follow 'im. See the idea? You could note where he goes, pop along and tell the perlice, and we'll nab the whole bloomin' bunch of these beauties!'

'It's a good idea, Jacob,' said Peter enthusiastically.

'Course it is,' chuckled the bookmaker. 'They gotta get up very early to get the better of old Jacob Bellamy!'

'You're going to draw this money from your bank,' asked the reporter, 'and have it ready when their messenger arrives?'

'Not on your bloomin' life, cock! I'm drawin' no money from my bank. There's a feller down at Greenwich — and I'm not telling you 'is name nor 'is address, so you needn't ask me — what can turn out quid notes that you couldn't tell from the real thing. He passed one on me once and that's 'ow I came to know 'im. But except for that he's a good feller. I'm goin' to get three thousand of 'is stock, and then if anythin' goes wrong I shan't be losin' nothin'. See?'

Peter smiled. It was characteristic of Jacob Bellamy that he should safeguard himself against loss. 'I think that's fine. I'm with you, Jacob, but I don't think we want anyone else.'

'No, p'raps you're right,' mumbled the other, his mouth full of a huge portion of steak and chips. 'I don't mind tellin' yer that I was thinkin' of gettin' a couple of the boys along, but p'raps the fewer people who know the better.'

'I think so,' said the reporter. 'We don't know who's in this racket, Jacob.'

'None of the old hands,' said the bookmaker confidently. 'They ain't got the nouse! The most they can do is to threaten a bookie with a beatin' up if he doesn't drop 'em a fiver. This is big business, but they ain't goin' to capitalise it from me,' he added. 'Now, don't you go and print a word in that paper of yours about me gettin' this letter or the fat'll be in the fire.'

'I shouldn't be such a fool.' Peter took a deep draught from his tankard. 'It'll be a colossal scoop if we can pull this off!' Already his mind was thinking in headlines: '*MORNING MAIL REPORTER PUTS AN END TO HORSESHOE MENACE.*'

'You get over to my place about ten on Monday,' said Mr. Bellamy. 'That'll give us time to prepare for this precious messenger. I'll fix up a place where you can 'ide, and I'll pretend to be all on me lonesome, see; a bit scared, like.' His eyes twinkled in their fleshy sockets. 'I'm glad they picked on me. This is goin' to give me the biggest kick I've 'ad for years!'

It was also going to give them both the biggest surprise they had ever had in their lives, but they did not know that then.

3

Superstitious Sam

Mr. Budd came out of the assistant commissioner's office in a black mood. It was not so much what Colonel Blair had actually said, as the way he said it, that had got beneath the stout man's skin; the more so since he knew he deserved the reprimand.

'This man came to us naturally expecting protection,' said the assistant commissioner acidly, 'and we failed to give it him. He acted in the way that any right-minded citizen should act, and he suffered for it with his life. He should never have been allowed to go from here without being watched. His death is a slur on the administration. I'll admit that this was an unprecedented case in this country, but that doesn't entirely excuse your handling of the matter. We should be prepared for unprecedented cases.'

Mr. Budd sat red-faced and silent, knowing the uselessness of attempting to justify himself.

'The killing of Arbinger will, naturally, shake people's faith in the ability of the police to offer protection in any similar circumstances,' continued Colonel Blair icily, 'and that means that we may receive no notification of the receipt of any other letters these Silver Horseshoe people send out. It will hamper us considerably in smashing this organisation. And it's got to be smashed, Superintendent! We owe it to the community at large, our own prestige, and John Arbinger, to see that the people responsible for his murder are apprehended within the shortest possible time. You have blundered badly, and if it was anybody else they would be given no chance to repeat that blunder. Your record is so good, however, that I don't propose to take you off the case. But I must have results. Please understand that!'

Feeling rather like a schoolboy who had been up before the head, Mr. Budd had left the office. As a consequence, the unfortunate Sergeant Leek found him more than unusually trying. 'Seen Blair?' he asked sympathetically when his superior came ponderously into his room.

Mr. Budd merely grunted, squeezing himself into his chair and mechanically taking one of his cigars from his pocket.

'What did he say?' inquired the lean sergeant curiously.

'We discussed the weather!' snarled the stout man, searching for his matches and biting the end of his cigar viciously.

'Oh, was that all?' Leek said disappointedly. 'I thought he sent for you for somethin' important. What did he want to talk about the weather for?'

'What d'you want to talk at all for?' snapped Mr. Budd irritably.

'Because I've got somethin' to say,' said the sergeant. 'I was readin' the other day that conversation's becomin' a lost art — '

'Well, don't try to find it!' interrupted his exasperated superior rudely. 'I want to think.' He closed his eyes and lay back in his chair, his cigar clenched between his teeth.

He realised that he was, to some extent,

to blame for the death of John Arbinger, and his fruitless endeavours to discover a clue to the bookmaker's murderers did nothing to alleviate his worried state of his mind. Although he had neglected nothing that might supply him with a line to the people behind the Horseshoe letters, he had been unsuccessful. All the recent American immigrants had been checked up without discovering one that could be implicated. The countless people who had been questioned concerning their whereabouts at the time of the killing had yielded nothing; and the car which, without doubt, had brought and taken away the murderers had not been found. The footprints which Divisional Inspector Bennet had been at such pains to retain for his inspection had so far proved useless as a clue. They had been made by shoes with plain rubber soles which, from the appearance of the prints, had been specially bought for the occasion.

There was just nothing to go on. The only chance at the moment lay in further activity on the part of the Silver

Horseshoe itself. If any more of the letters were sent out and the recipients communicated with the Yard, then he would be supplied with a fresh beginning. But it was unlikely that anyone would come forward. Fear of the consequences would keep them silent.

For an hour he sat smoking and thinking, and then putting on his hat he growled a word to the melancholy Leek and went out to the little tea shop round the corner, where he usually took his frugal lunch.

The place was crowded, but his table had been kept for him and he sat down, pushing his hard derby hat to the back of his head. The girl who always served him smiled a greeting and went away to attend to his order, which never varied: two rounds of buttered toast and a pot of tea.

He was pouring out his first cup of tea when a man came through the swing doors and stood for a moment looking about him. He was short and stout, and jovial-faced, with little twinkling eyes that shone brightly from behind a pair of hornrimmed spectacles. He caught sight of the table at which the big superintendent was sitting, and coming over dropped into the vacant chair opposite him.

Mr. Budd gave him a casual glance, noting more from habit than interest the plump, well-kept hands, the expensive tweed overcoat, and the glittering ring that ornamented one of the fat fingers.

'Lucky to find an empty seat,' said the newcomer cheerfully. 'Most of these places are full up at this hour.'

The big man grunted. He was not at all pleased at having a loquacious companion thrust on him.

'I guess luck plays a big part in people's lives,' went on the other, with the faintest trace of an American accent. 'I'm a great believer in luck.'

He turned to give an order to the waitress, who had come up and was standing at his elbow expectantly; and Mr. Budd, who cared very little what he believed in, began to munch one of his pieces of toast stolidly.

'Yes, I'm a great believer in luck,' repeated the stout little man when the girl had gone to execute his order. 'My friends call me 'Superstitious Sam'. I wouldn't walk under a ladder or open an umbrella in the house or pass a horseshoe without picking it up. I'm particularly superstitious about horseshoes.'

Mr. Budd's moving jaw ceased abruptly and his sleepy eyes opened a little wider. The man had spoken quite naturally. There was no emphasis on the 'horseshoe', but the eyes behind the glasses were regarding him searchingly.

The stout superintendent stiffened. 'That's very interesting sir,' he murmured noncommittally.

'It's surprising,' went on the little man blandly, 'what a lot of superstitious people there are in the racing world.' The waitress set down a cup of coffee and a bun in front of him and he beamed his thanks. 'I know quite a lot of punters and bookmakers who go in for charms,' he continued. 'Black cats and lucky beans, and sometimes . . . silver horseshoes.' He was staring deliberately at Mr. Budd as he spoke, a broad smile on his round face.

'Silver horseshoes, eh?' said the stout superintendent, stirring his tea slowly. 'Well now, that's funny, 'cause I've been hearin' a lot about silver horseshoes lately.'

'Have you, now?' The man who called himself 'Superstitious Sam' raised surprised eyebrows. 'That's mighty peculiar — what some people'd call a coincidence, don't you think?'

'Some people might,' said Mr. Budd warily. 'I'm not a believer in coincidences myself.'

His companion took a sip at his coffee. 'I think you're wise,' he said. 'Maybe you agree with me that horseshoes aren't always lucky, eh?'

'Maybe. What's all this leadin' to?'

The other cut his bun in half methodically. 'What you're wondering,' he said calmly, 'is who the heck I am, and what I've been saying has got to do with the death of John Arbinger. Isn't that right?'

'Well, it did cross my mind,' admitted Mr. Budd. 'Supposin' you tell me, instead of shootin' all this stuff about luck and superstition?'

'That's not an unreasonable request,' said the little man, carefully buttering his bun. 'My name's Samuel K. Piggott, and I'm a citizen of the United States of America. Possibly you guessed that.'

'I guessed the American part of it,' murmured the superintendent. 'Go on. You're gettin' to the interestin' bit now.'

'I read about the murder of Arbinger and the horseshoe letters in the *Evening Comet*,' continued Mr. Piggott, 'and I was curious. It said that you were in charge of the case and I thought I'd like to make your acquaintance.'

'So you guessed I was in the habit of coming here and followed me,' said Mr. Budd, 'or did you just choose this place and trust to luck?'

The round face in front of him creased into a broad smile. 'I knew you were in here because I saw you come in,' retorted the little man. 'I've been standing on the opposite side of the street for the last hour for just that purpose.'

'And now you've got to know me,' said

51

the stout superintendent, 'what then?'

The smile vanished from the American's face and he leaned forward earnestly. 'This,' he answered seriously. 'Be careful! These 'Horseshoe' people are dangerous — how dangerous you've yet to realise. You've had no experience of this kind of racket over here. It was born and bred in America. This is the first time it's crossed the Atlantic. You can't handle it with kid gloves.'

'I never wear 'em,' said the big man. 'See here, Mr. Piggott, just what *do* you know about this business?'

'Nothing, but I guess a lot,' answered Piggott quickly. 'And my guesses remain my own property.' He was once more the bland, genial man who had first come in. 'Maybe we shall see quite a lot of each other in the future.'

'It seems quite likely,' said Mr. Budd significantly. 'Yes, I should think it was very likely.'

The little man chuckled. 'You're wondering whether you ought to arrest me straight away as a suspicious character,' he said. 'But it won't do you any good. You've got nothing against me, and you wouldn't be able to hold me.'

'I'm not goin' to do anythin' so foolish,' Mr. Budd said, shaking his head. 'But I would like to know just why you've gone to all this trouble.'

'My reason is a personal one,' he said slowly. 'The time is coming — sooner or later — when we may be of mutual assistance to each other.'

'How?' asked Mr. Budd.

'You'll know when the time comes,' declared Mr. Piggott emphatically. 'Yes, sir! You'll know!'

★　★　★

Peter Ashton rented a little cottage in a fold of the Berkshire Hills to which he was in the habit of retiring whenever the exigencies of his profession permitted. It consisted of two rooms: a tiny kitchen, and a bath which he had had inexpensively installed. The boundary of Lord Sevenways's fine estate touched the small garden, and the cottage was approached by a winding lane which opened off the main thoroughfare half a mile below the lodge gates.

On the Saturday night following his interview with Mr. Jacob Bellamy, Peter took out his shabby little car and drove down to this haven of rest, glad of the opportunity which the weekend offered for getting away from the bustle and turmoil of Fleet Street. He had a lot to think about, and the quiet of the country in late spring was an excellent background. He went to bed early and spent Sunday lazily in his small garden, wondering what the Monday night would bring forth, and whether old Jacob's plan would lead to any result. Peter experienced a thrill of anticipation at the prospect of being led to the fountainhead of the organisation. It would be a tremendous scoop for the *Morning Mail*, and an additional feather in his already well-plumed hat.

He returned to London in the early hours of Monday morning, and his first action on reaching his flat in Gray's Inn Road was to telephone the bookmaker.

'Listen, Jacob. About tonight. I think

ten o'clock is a bit late for me to come along. They'll probably have someone watching your house, and if I'm seen going in they'll get suspicious.'

'Maybe you're right, boy. Whatcher goin' to do, then?'

'I'm coming at seven,' said the reporter, 'and I'm coming by the back way. Isn't there a little alley at the foot of your garden?'

'There is,' replied Jacob. 'It runs along the end of my garden and divides the others that back on to it.'

'Then look out for me that way,' said Peter, and rang off.

After a quick breakfast, he walked down to his office and interviewed Mr. Sorbet. Jacob Bellamy had been averse to the news editor being taken into their confidence, but on Peter's assurance that nothing would be printed that might endanger the scheme, had rather reluctantly consented.

'I think it's a wise move,' said Mr. Sorbet with a fiendish scowl, when Peter had explained the slight alteration he had made in the arrangement. 'You've got the chance of your life, Ashton. Don't bungle it! I'm expecting a big story from this.'

The promise of the sunny morning was not fulfilled, for during the afternoon it clouded over and at six o'clock, when Peter went to the garage where he kept his small car, it had begun to rain. He had decided to drive to Bellamy's house and leave his car in one of the quiet roads nearby. There was every possibility that the messenger of the 'Horseshoe' would not come on foot, and without the car Peter would be at a disadvantage.

It was raining in torrents when he reached Wimbledon and sought out Mr. Bellamy's villa. It was a small semi-detached house standing in a road of similar houses. Peter passed the end of the turning and brought his car to a halt in the deserted street into which the entrance to the alley he had spoken of emerged. Leaving the machine, he turned up the collar of his macintosh and walked slowly back towards the narrow opening which gave admittance to the little paved walk, keeping a sharp lookout for anyone who might be lurking in the vicinity. But he saw nobody, and concluded that if the house was being watched, the watcher was confining his attentions to the front.

He passed along between the high fences and presently came to the end of Mr. Bellamy's garden. There was a narrow door which gave admittance to the alley, and he found it unlocked. He slipped through, closing the door after him, and after a moment's hesitation shot the bolt.

The little garden was gay with spring flowers, but Peter had no time to waste in admiration. Walking quickly up one of the well-kept paths, he made his way towards the house. The garden was so arranged that rustic screens covered with rambling roses hid the back entrance from the view of anyone skirting the tiny lawn.

The water was dripping from his hat when he reached the green-painted back door and knocked softly on the little brass knocker. The door was opened almost immediately.

'Come in, cock,' greeted the husky voice of Mr. Bellamy. 'Leave your hat and coat out here.'

Peter removed the dripping garment and hung it together with his hat on a peg behind the door.

'We're all on our own,' continued the bookmaker, 'so you'll have to be content with cold grub. I sent the woman away as soon as she'd laid the table.' He led the way through a spotless kitchen, along a passage, and into a pleasant little dining room. 'What'll you have?' he said, going over to the sideboard.

'I'll have a sherry,' said Peter, and while the bookmaker filled two glasses went over to the window and cautiously looked out. It faced the street, and he peered at the deserted thoroughfare, but there was nobody in sight.

'Looking to see if the place is being watched?' said Mr. Bellamy, holding out a glass.

'Yes,' Peter answered as he took it. 'But I don't think it is. I couldn't see anybody at the back, either.'

'I looked, too,' said old Jacob, 'when I came in, and I didn't see no one. Well, cheerio, cock!' He raised his glass. 'Here's luck.' He swallowed half the contents at a gulp, and set the glass down on a corner of the table. 'I've got everythin' fixed up,' he went on. 'Went down and saw that feller I spoke about yesterday, and collected the goods. I'll show 'em to you after we've eaten.'

'I suppose you know you could be pinched?' said Peter severely.

'I've been in danger of bein' pinched too many times in my life, cock,' he chuckled, 'to worry much about that. Let's eat.'

He finished the rest of his sherry, waved Peter to a chair, and took his place at the table. When they had finished the meal he suggested an adjournment to his study, and they crossed the little hall to the comfortable, untidy apartment.

It was a cosy room, full of photographs and relics of Mr. Bellamy's chequered career, and the principal article of furniture consisted of a huge roll-top desk that stood in an angle by the window. The bookmaker crossed over to this, pulled open a drawer, and took out a thick packet.

'There y'are, boy,' he said, throwing it

into Peter's lap. 'Three thousand quid, and every one of 'em 'slush'.'

The reporter examined the bundle curiously. Mr. Bellamy's mysterious friend was undoubtedly an artist, for unless he'd been told beforehand, he would never have guessed the notes were not the genuine article.

'They ought to fool 'em,' said old Jacob complacently, and Peter agreed. 'And here's another thing for you while I think of it,' said the bookmaker, rummaging in the same drawer from which he had taken the notes. 'You'd better have this, just in case of trouble.' He held out a squat, ugly-looking automatic pistol, and Peter took it. 'Be careful,' warned Bellamy. 'It's loaded, and there's a cartridge in the breach.'

Peter slipped the weapon into his pocket. 'Have you got a licence for this?' he inquired, and Bellamy shook his head.

'No, cock,' he answered. 'Nor for this, neither.' He took out a second pistol. 'I borrowed 'em from a friend of mine.'

'I can see us getting two years over this business,' remarked Peter with a sigh.

'You seem to have broken most of the laws of the country already.'

'The laws of the country mean nothin' to me, boy,' said Mr. Bellamy, dismissing them with a wave of a huge hand. 'Not when it comes to dealin' with people like these 'Horseshoe' beggars. When you come up against a lot of thugs that fight foul you don't want to worry too much about stickin' to the Queensberry rules.' He looked at his watch. 'Half past eight,' he murmured. 'I don't suppose anything'll happen till midnight, when they said, but we'd better start preparing round about eleven. That means we've got about two hours and a half to fill in. Have a drink?' Without waiting for Peter's reply, he poured out two generous portions.

'There's cigars on that table beside yer,' he said, helping himself to one as he spoke. 'We can stop in here and chat until eleven, and then I think you'd better make yourself scarce, boy. There's a little lobby in the hall an' if you slip in there you'll be able to see who arrives and follow 'em when they leave.'

61

Old Jacob Bellamy had a fund of stories and anecdotes, and Peter became so interested in his apparently inexhaustible experiences that he almost forgot the real reason for his visit. It was with something like surprise that he saw the bookmaker suddenly rise to his feet.

'Time we got busy, cock,' said old Jacob. 'It's just eleven.' He opened the door and Peter followed him out into the hall.

The lobby he had mentioned was on the right, a tiny room where Mr. Bellamy kept his hat and overcoat.

'Here y'are, boy,' he said. 'If you leave the door ajar you can see the hall, an' I'll put the light on.' He went over and pressed down the switch. 'Now I think everything's set,' he remarked. 'When this feller arrives I'll take him into the study. You can slip out by the door and wait for him comin' out.'

Peter shook his head. 'He may have somebody with him,' he objected. 'No; what I'll do, Jacob, is to leave by the back way and collect my car. You can keep the man long enough to enable me to get round to the front. If he comes by car I shall be ready for him. If he doesn't I can leave mine and follow him on foot.'

'OK,' said Mr. Bellamy. 'Now I'm goin' to take up my well-known role of a spider.'

He went back to the study and Peter settled down to wait, the door of the little cloakroom open an inch so that he could see the front door and nearly all of the hall.

It was still raining heavily; he could hear the patter of it on the window behind him and the gurgle of the gutters. Twice the sound of wheels from the street outside arrested his attention, but they faded into silence, testifying that they had no connection with the thing he was awaiting.

The minutes slowly passed, then a soft whirr and a muffled bell from somewhere in the silent house told him that a clock was beginning to strike twelve. The last note died away, and as it did so there came an uncertain knock on the front door. Peter's heart leaped and he almost held his breath.

The knock was repeated, and Mr. Bellamy came out of his study, passed across the reporter's line of vision, and fumbled with the catch. The front door swung open under his hand and Peter, with his eyes glued to the crack of the cloakroom door, waited tensely to see who would enter.

He heard a murmured whisper and saw the huge form of old Bellamy start. Then, as he stood aside, a slim figure came hesitantly into the light of the pendant which hung from the ceiling. Peter saw the shining green raincoat, the little green hat, and the white face beneath, and caught his breath in a gasp of astonishment. The messenger was Marjorie Arbinger!

4

The Compact

Peter blinked incredulously. Marjorie Arbinger — the daughter of the man who had been shot down in cold blood as an example! It was impossible . . . and yet there she stood, obviously nervous and ill at ease, while old Jacob Bellamy stared down at her, his ugly face almost ludicrous in its expression of astonishment.

'You — you have something for me?' She spoke in a low voice, but Peter heard every word.

The bookmaker's face hardened. 'You've come from these Silver Horseshoe people?' he demanded harshly.

'The Silver Horseshoe?' she repeated wonderingly, and shook her head. 'No, Mr. Bellamy. I came because of this!' She fumbled in the pocket of her raincoat and produced an envelope which she handed to the old man. He took it suspiciously, frowned at the inscription, and raised his eyebrows.

'Are you Miss Arbinger, John Arbinger's daughter?' he exclaimed in amazement.

'Yes,' she answered.

'Well, this beats me,' he muttered, and inserting a thumb and finger drew out a sheet of paper. As he read the letter his face changed; the harshness faded and was replaced by a look of perplexity. 'When did you get this?' he asked.

'This morning,' she replied. 'Didn't you write it?'

He shook his head. 'No, miss. Is this why you came?'

'Yes, of course,' she said. 'For what other reason would I come at this hour?'

Bellamy turned helplessly towards the door of the little cloakroom.

'You'd better come out, boy,' he called. Peter had already left his hiding place, to the amazement of the girl, who stared at his sudden appearance in blank astonishment. 'Look at that, and see if you can make head or tail of it. I can't!' Mr. Bellamy thrust the letter into Peter's hands and the reporter scanned it swiftly:

15, Oak Apple Road,
Wimbledon.
May 11th.
    'Dear Miss Arbinger,
'I was a friend of your late father's
and am in a position to give you
certain information regarding the
people responsible for his unfortu-
nate and tragic death. Please call at
the above address at twelve midnight
on Monday, the 12th. Come alone,
and come exactly at the time I have
mentioned. You may be surprised at
this stipulation, but believe me
circumstances make it imperative. If
you wish to see your father's
murderers pay the penalty for their
crime do not fail to come.
    Yours sincerely,
    Jacob Bellamy.'

With the exception of the signature the
letter was typewritten.

    'This is not your signature?' said Peter.
    'Of course it isn't, boy!' Jacob declared.

'I never wrote the thing. I know nothing about it!'

The girl looked from one to the other in bewilderment. 'Then — then what does it mean?' she asked.

'It means that they've had us for a lot of mugs!' replied the reporter bitterly. 'You got this this morning, Miss Arbinger?'

'Yes,' she said. 'By the first post. I was a little astonished, but I've heard Daddy talk about Mr. Bellamy and I thought perhaps there might be something in it. You see, I'd give anything to find out who — who killed him.' There was a trace of huskiness in her voice.

'So would I, Miss Arbinger,' said Peter grimly, 'and I was hoping we might have got somewhere near tonight.'

'You're Mr. Ashton, aren't you?' she said. 'The reporter who came to interview me?' And when Peter nodded: 'What are you doing here?' Her eyes strayed from Peter to the burly figure of the old bookmaker. 'If you didn't write that letter, why was it you were expecting me?'

'I wasn't expecting you, miss,' he

growled. 'I was expecting somebody quite different.'

'Let's go into your study, Jacob,' said Peter quickly, 'and explain the situation to Miss Arbinger. I think she's entitled to know.'

'What about our scheme?' said Jacob.

'That's gone west!' said the reporter. 'These Horseshoe people got wind of our idea somehow and sent Miss Arbinger instead of the messenger we expected. They're probably laughing up their sleeve at the way we've been had!'

'I don't see how they could have found out,' growled Bellamy. His famous plan had fizzled out like a damp squib, and he was not unnaturally disappointed.

'Well, let's go into the study,' he said, and led the way into the cosy room.

'You're very wet,' said Peter, as the girl was preparing to follow. 'Don't you think you'd better slip your raincoat off?' She hesitated, and then complied. 'It'll dry while we're talking,' he said, taking it from her and hanging it on a hook inside the lobby, 'and I can drive you back.'

He shepherded her into the study and

settled her in an easy chair before the dying fire. The hospitable Mr. Bellamy offered drinks, but she shook her head. 'No, thank you,' she said. 'I'll have a cigarette, though, if I may.'

Peter hastily supplied her with one, and when he had lit it took upon himself the duty of explaining what had led up to this surprising denouement. She listened attentively, and when he had finished looked over at old Jacob.

'So you got one of these letters, too,' she said.

'I did, miss,' he grunted, 'and I thought I was going to be clever. I still don't see how they could have found out about my plan — I ain't told a soul!'

'I wonder what their object was in bringing me here?' said the girl thoughtfully, and Peter made no reply.

That was worrying him. If they'd known what Bellamy and he had arranged between them, why had they taken this means of retaliating? It was hardly likely that so much trouble would have been taken without a serious purpose, and this aspect worried him. It would have been so much easier to have just left things instead of arranging for the girl to appear at the exact hour when the messenger was expected.

It was Bellamy who broke the awkward silence that had descended upon them.

'Well, they've played us for a couple of suckers, boy!' said the old man. 'And Miss Arbinger, too. But I haven't finished with 'em yet. Nobody's going to make a fool of Jacob Bellamy and get away with it!'

'Let me help,' Marjorie said eagerly. 'I'd do anything, anything I could! Daddy never did anyone any harm and — and I saw him just after — ' The tears welled up in her eyes and the old bookmaker crossed over and patted her shoulder.

'There, there, my dear,' he said. 'Don't think about it. I knew John Arbinger. One of the best men that ever lived. And if I can get my hands on the people who killed him there won't be much left of 'em. I'm going to find the people at the back of the 'Horseshoe' ... even if it costs me every penny I've got!'

Peter caught sight of the look on his

face and believed him.

'But you don't want to get mixed up in it,' he went on. 'You keep clear. This isn't a woman's job.'

'I'm not afraid.' She looked from one to the other, and seeing the doubt on their faces went on rapidly: 'You think because I'm only a girl I wouldn't be any use, but there's lots of things I could do, lots of ways in which I might be able to help.'

'It's not that we don't think you'd be any use,' said Peter gravely, 'but these people are dangerous murderers, Miss Arbinger.'

'All the more reason why they should be stamped out,' she interrupted.

'The police — ' began Peter, but she stopped him with a contemptuous gesture.

'Daddy went to the police and they let him be killed. Mr. Bellamy, you say you're willing to spend every penny you've got to find these people. Let me help. I've got money, too. Daddy left everything to me. Let me help. It will give me a new interest in life, stop me brooding.'

'No, no, child,' said old Jacob, shaking

his head. 'No, Miss Arbinger, you must keep out of this.'

'I won't!' she said, and stamped her foot. 'If you won't let me help you I'll work on my own, and that'll be far more dangerous than if I had you two behind me. I've thought about it before. Why do you think I came in answer to that letter? Because I thought there was a possibility of learning something concerning the people who killed Daddy.'

'But — ' protested Peter, but she refused to listen.

'There are no 'buts',' she said. 'You and I and Mr. Bellamy can fight these people. Surely we've got as many brains between us as they have? Let's fight them — and crush them!'

There was a silence, and she waited, breathing quickly.

'I'll agree, on one condition,' said Jacob, and Peter knew it was the threat of working on her own that had won him over. 'And that is that you do nothing without consulting us.'

'I'll accept your condition,' she retorted, 'provided you make a similar promise, and also that you allow me to put up half the expenses.'

'No, no!' argued Bellamy. 'That's my pigeon.'

'Very well,' she said reluctantly. Then she smiled for the first time since he had arrived. 'It's settled then. The three of us work together against the murderers of my father.'

''One for all and all for one',' quoted Peter. 'Though I think we're up against a tougher proposition than anything the three Musketeers ever tackled. And now, Miss Arbinger,' he went on, 'I'm going to take you home. It's after one o'clock and we can't do anything tonight. We'll meet tomorrow and discuss a plan of campaign.'

The girl nodded. 'Come and have tea with me,' she suggested; and this was agreed upon.

Peter fetched her coat, and the bookmaker accompanied them into the hall. 'I think it's stopped raining,' he said as he opened the door. 'Yes, it's a fine night now.'

'Wait here, Miss Arbinger, while I go

and find my car,' said Peter. 'It's — '

He broke off as he caught sight of something white attached to one of the panels. It was a square of paper, pinned below the knocker with a drawing pin. On it were three lines of typewritten writing:

'John Arbinger defied us and died. You will suffer the same fate unless you are wise.'

Beneath was the stamped impression of the silver horseshoe.

Jacob Bellamy snatched the offending message down and crumpled it up in his huge hand. 'So much for that!' he said. 'I'm not afraid of them or their threats!'

'All the same,' said Peter gravely, 'you've got to be careful, Jacob.'

'It'll take more than a bunch of crooks to scare me, boy!' he growled. 'Now be off, you two.'

The girl was silent as they turned out of the little street and headed towards London, and Peter thought she had fallen asleep, until suddenly she raised her head.

'I like Mr. Bellamy,' she said. 'I hope nothing happens to him.'

Peter hoped so, too. He was far from

easy in his mind regarding the old bookmaker, although he kept his fears to himself. Nothing was more certain, in his opinion, than that the Silver Horseshoe would follow their threat with action.

That he was justified in this conviction was proved before the next forty-eight hours had passed.

* * *

Of all the dark and dingy London streets, Tilbury Street is the darkest and the dingiest. It runs between two main thoroughfares, and is so narrow that the tall office buildings which line its pavements seem almost to touch. The buildings are mostly divided into small suites of offices occupied by commercial firms of integrity, whose combined income tax provides an appreciable addition to the funds of the country.

On the top floor of one of the cramped, smoke-grimed old buildings, and approached by a tortuous stairway, is a door bearing the inscription in startlingly new white letters: J. Stanmore, Limited.

J. Stanmore is evidently a newcomer, and something of a mystery to his fellow tenants, for the office which he rents is never open during the daytime, and no sign of life has ever been seen during traditional business hours. Whatever is transacted in the office of J. Stanmore, Limited takes place during those hours when ordinary business firms have closed down.

J. Stanmore has no callers. The crooked stairway which leads up to his suite remains deserted. The company employs no staff, and the man who comes under cover of darkness and stays until midnight is never seen by the more conservative occupants whose day's work ends with the striking of six.

Tilbury Street, after the cleaners have left, is a deserted wilderness, and remains so until the activities of the day begin, shortly after eight. On a wet night it is a drear and miserable locality — a lonely waste given over to stray cats who creep furtively in the gutters or lurk silently in the dark entrances.

The rain was falling heavily and a clock

had just finished chiming the hour of ten when a man in a shining black mackintosh came swiftly along the main thoroughfare and turned into the deserted stretch of Tilbury Street. His chin was buried in a muffler and the brim of his dripping hat was pulled low over his eyes so that very little of his face was visible, even if there had been anyone there to see.

He strode rapidly along the narrow pavement until he came to a closed door, two thirds of the way down the street, and here he stopped. From the pocket of his waterproof he produced a bunch of keys, selected one, and inserted it in the lock. A second later the door had opened and closed and Tilbury Street was once more deserted.

In the narrow passage beyond, the man produced a torch and directed its white rays on the uncarpeted stairway that led into the shadows above. Silently he began to mount, passing floor after floor until he came to the door giving admittance to the offices of J. Stanmore, Limited. Once more the bunch of keys was brought out and he let himself in, shutting and locking the door behind him. When he had done this he pocketed his torch, and pressing a switch put on a dim light that came from a dusty bulb in the centre of the ceiling.

The suite consisted of two rooms, an outer and an inner office, with a communicating door between. The outer room was bare and unfurnished, except for a counter that ran from wall to wall, with a flap at one end. The late visitor removed his coat and hat and hung them on a rack that had been screwed into one wall, and crossing to the door of the inner room unlocked it and passed through. When he had switched on the light here he came back and put out the other.

The inner office was better furnished. A large, flat-topped table occupied the centre, its surface bare except for a blotting pad, a calendar and an inkstand. There was a shabby armchair drawn up by the empty grate and a revolving desk chair behind the table. In one corner, on a plain deal table, stood a duplicating machine. A filing cabinet occupied the space behind the door. All the furniture was old, and the shabby square of carpet which only partially covered the bare boards did nothing to remove the appearance of poverty which the place suggested.

The man who had come to this dismal office at such an unusual time sat down in the chair behind the centre table, and after lighting a cigarette unlocked a drawer and produced a small red leather book which he consulted. It consisted of a list of names and addresses, against some of which was a cross in red ink. He studied this for some time, and then laying it aside, still open, he took from the same drawer a letter and read it carefully. After he had done so he compared it with the book, picked up a pen from the tray in front of him, dipped it in the ink, and made six more crosses against an equivalent number of names in the record.

Blotting his additions, he took out his watch, laid it on the table in front of him, and from a second drawer produced a series of duplicated sheets. With another pen, using black ink this time, he filled in the blank spaces, constantly referring to the letter at his elbow as he did so. And when the last one had been completed he folded them, brought out six typewritten envelopes, and enclosed the sheets, licking down the flaps. These he replaced in the drawer and carefully locked it.

His cigarette had burnt itself out in a tray in front of him, and lighting another he sat back in his chair, and for several minutes stared thoughtfully at the dingy ceiling. The first part of the night's task was done. The time for the second was not yet ripe. Presently he roused himself, eyed the telephone, and put away the book and the letter.

It was five minutes to eleven when the silence of the room was broken by a soft-toned buzzer. The man at the table leaned forward and picked up the receiver. 'Yes?' he said, and listened to the voice that came over the wire. 'You saw her catch the train? You're sure of that? Well, that's all for tonight. Ring up at the usual hour tomorrow.'

He put the instrument back on its rack, made a note on a slip of paper, and once more leaned back in his chair. Three minutes passed, and then the buzzer went again.

'Yes?' he called. 'Oh, it's you. Listen — these are your instructions. You will proceed to Wimbledon, timing it so that you reach there shortly after twelve, taking with you the paper that was sent you this morning. You will go to Fifteen Oak Apple Road and pin the paper on the front door, taking every precaution to avoid being seen. That is all. Report tomorrow at the usual time.'

Once again he rang off, and this time he had barely done so when a third call came through. They followed thick and fast, and for the next hour there was scarcely an interval between them. It was just on midnight when he dealt with the last and stretched himself. The slip of paper before him was covered with notes, and picking this up he read it through carefully, pulled the telephone towards him and gave a number. This was the final and most important part of his duties.

'Hello!' he called, when a voice at the other end assured him that he was connected with the person he wished to speak to. 'This is Mark. Yes, everything's all right. I've attended to everything. The girl fell for the letter. Yes . . . Yes . . . At the present moment we've collected five thousand pounds. Bellamy will be dealt with as you suggested. Yes, I've already arranged with Sellini. I don't think we shall have any trouble with the others at all. Two have paid up, as I told you, and I think the rest will fall into line. What about the reporter? I think he may be troublesome.' There was an interval of silence while he listened to the comments that the other had to make. 'Well perhaps,' he said, 'we can discuss that when we meet. There's no immediate hurry. The other letters are all ready to go out as soon as we've cleared up the last batch. Yes. I think that's all. Good night.'

He laid the receiver slowly down and rose to his feet. His work for that day was over. Passing out into the outer office he pulled on his waterproof, switched on the light, and returning to the inner room gave a quick glance round. The keys were still in one of the drawers of the desk and he clicked his teeth impatiently as he saw how near he had been to forgetting them. Dropping them into his pocket he switched out the light, felt his way to the door, and shut it behind him.

Three minutes later he was in the street and locking the outer door. As he straightened up from this he saw the burly form of a policeman coming towards him. The constable slowed and glanced suspiciously as he drew level.

'Didn't you come out of that building just now?' he inquired gruffly.

The man in the waterproof nodded. 'Yes, it's all right, officer. I've got an office there,' he said. 'Been working late. Stanmore, my name is — of Stanmore, Limited.' He groped in his pocket, produced a wallet, and extracted a card which he held out to the policeman.

The man took it, looked at the inscription by the light of his lantern, and his face cleared. 'Sorry, sir,' he said apologetically. 'But it's unusual to see anybody about so late as this in these parts. We have to be careful.'

'Quite right, too,' said the man who

called himself Stanmore. 'Good night.'

'Good night, sir,' said the policeman, and continued on his way, unaware of the chance of promotion which fate had dangled before his eyes.

For the man who was walking rapidly down Tilbury Street was the 'right hand' of the unknown whose identity was concealed under the symbol of a silver horseshoe.

5

The Razor Boys

The conference which was held at Marjorie Arbinger's house between Peter, the girl and Jacob Bellamy on the Tuesday afternoon was not very successful in forwarding the campaign against the 'Silver Horshoe'. Peter summed up the situation fairly accurately after they had discussed the matter from every angle for over two hours.

'We can do nothing at all at the present juncture,' he declared. 'We've got nothing to catch hold of. The people working this racket are unknown, and until they make a further move they're likely to remain so. All we can hope for is that they'll have another go at Jacob. That might give us the lead we want.'

'We've just gotta be patient,' said old Jacob. 'I've got a hunch that something'll turn up before long, an' in the old days my hunches were as good as cast-iron certainties.'

'I suppose you're right,' said the girl. 'But I wish we could do something.'

She tried to persuade them to stay to dinner, but Bellamy had already arranged to meet a friend at his club, and Peter had to return to his office to clear up some work which he had left to keep the girl's invitation.

'Nice gal, that,' remarked Mr. Bellamy as he prepared to get into his car.

'Very,' agreed Peter.

'If I'd ever married and 'ad children,' continued the old man, 'that's the kind of daughter I'd like to have had. Maybe she'll make someone a good wife one of these days. Well, so long, cock. I'll keep in touch with you.' He waved a huge hand, and the reporter watched his car disappear down Putney Hill before seeking his own.

On his way to Fleet Street the words of old Jacob persisted in running through his mind, until he found himself thinking such dangerous thoughts that he abruptly switched to the work that lay awaiting him.

Mr. Bellamy spent a pleasant evening at his club, which numbered many of his old cronies amongst its membership, and set off home shortly before eleven in a complacent mood.

He garaged his car in the main thoroughfare, which was about five minutes' walk from his little villa, and when he had handed it over to the man in charge set off to cover the distance on foot.

He had turned into his quiet street when, without the least warning, he was surrounded by half a dozen men who seemed to spring from nowhere. Instantly on the alert, he stopped, his huge fists clenched. 'Now then, what's the game?' he demanded.

'The game's a little timely warning, Bellamy,' said a flashily dressed man who appeared to be their leader. 'You know me, eh?'

'I know you all right, Sellini,' growled Jacob, his jaw setting. 'Bit out of your district, isn't it?'

'Never mind about districts,' snarled Tony Sellini. 'We've got you proper,

Bellamy, and by the time we've finished with you your own mother won't know you. Go on, boys, beat him up!'

'It'd take more than a gang of race-course toughs to do that!' growled Bellamy, and lashing out with his right caught the leering face in front of him a smashing blow on the point of the prominent jaw. In spite of his age Bellamy's punch was like the kick of an ox, and Sellini went down, to sprawl whimpering on the pavement.

The sudden and unexpected attack on their leader disconcerted the others for a moment, but only for a moment; and then with a rush they came upon the bookmaker, and he turned to meet the onslaught. A razor flashed viciously near his face. He ducked, caught the wielder of the weapon round the waist, and hurled him into the middle of his companions.

The action gained him a second's respite and he took advantage of it to get his back against the blank wall of the house near which the attack had come. And then he was in the midst of a mass of whirling arms and flashing blades. One sleeve of his overcoat was ripped to rags; the knuckles of his hands were raw and bleeding, but he continued to fight, planting his blows unerringly.

Tony Sellini scrambled to his feet, muttering lurid oaths and holding his aching jaw, but he made no attempt to take further part in the fight, contenting himself by hovering about on the edge of the melee, grunting instructions.

Bellamy smashed a bunched fist into a face that came within range and sent its owner staggering into the arms of two of his friends. They shouldered him away, and he fell ungracefully, rolling over and over into the gutter.

Up to that moment the old man was holding his own, but he realised that he couldn't do so for long. The odds against him were eight to one. Sooner or later the vicious razors would inflict a serious wound, and then . . .

His eyes, wary and watchful, flickered about him and saw something that might turn the scales in his favour. On the corner of the street stood the red pillar of a fire-alarm. If he could reach that . . .

With the idea came a glimmer of hope. A razor came swishing past his neck and he caught the wrist of the man who held it, giving the arm a sharp jerk. There was a crack and a squeal of pain as the joint dislocated. Stooping quickly, he gripped one of the attacker's ankles, and with a prodigious effort swung the screaming man up over his head. For a second he was held there struggling, and then hurled full at the others who had concentrated on an ugly rush. The impact sent them back off their feet and gained for Bellamy the advantage he had looked for to put his plan into execution.

Panting heavily, the old man darted towards the fire alarm, smashed the glass, and tugged at the handle. A warning cry came from the injured Sellini as he saw what had happened. 'Beat it, boys!' he shouted. 'The old so-and-so's done us!'

The warning took effect. The fallen members of the gang scrambled to their feet and hurried after the retreating forms of their companions. Sellini was following when a hand gripped him by the collar.

'No you don't, cock!' growled Mr.

Bellamy breathlessly. 'I want to have a word with you!'

His captive struggled violently as he was dragged along towards the alley that ran along the back of the row of houses in which he lived.

As he entered the narrow way a jangling bell warned him that the fire brigade which he had summoned were on their way.

Spitting curses and trying desperately to release himself, Sellini was propelled along in front of the old man and flung through the gate into the garden.

'Now!' said Jacob Bellamy. 'You and me's goin' to have a little talk, see. And by the time I've finished you'll wish you'd never been born — if you ever were.'

The amount of malignancy which he infused into his tone brought a look of alarm to the bruised face of his captive. Like all his kind he was a coward at heart, and without the support of his satellites was no longer the blustering bully that he had been.

But fear gave Mr. Sellini the courage of desperation. He sprang at the old man, lashing out wildly, but his fist met empty air, and the next second he was sprawling on his back, his nose feeling as though it had been broken. Bellamy dragged him to his feet and twisted his wrist, forcing his arm up behind his back so that he couldn't move without breaking it. He began whimpering with pain and terror as he was marched up towards the house. The bookmaker flung open the back door and thrust his prisoner into the kitchen with such force that he fell up against the table and slid to the floor.

'Now,' said the bookmaker, 'who put you up to this, eh?' He stooped, gripped his victim by the opening of his waistcoat and jerked him to his feet.

'Nobody!' whimpered Sellini. 'Give over, Mr. Bellamy.'

But the old man's reply was to shake him like a rat until his teeth rattled. 'You'll tell me what I want to know,' he said between his teeth, 'or you'll leave here a mass of pulp. Now then, who was behind it?'

'I'll see you in Hell first!' snarled Sellini with a sudden dash of spirit.

'Right! Then don't blame me for what happens to yer,' answered Bellamy. He released his grip so suddenly that the gang leader went stumbling back against the table, and began calmly to remove his coat and jacket and lay both garments across the back of a chair. 'I'm goin' to beat you up until you either talk or become just one big bruise.'

Sellini's breath left him in a gasp as the other began methodically to roll up his shirt sleeves. He glanced wildly about him like a trapped animal, but he said nothing. The bookmaker shot out a huge hand, gripped his coat, and with one wrench tore it from him. The action was so brutal that it broke the last remnant of Sellini's nerve.

'All right!' he almost sobbed. 'I'll tell you all I know.'

'Come on then, let's hear it!' snapped the bookmaker.

'It was a feller I've never seen before,' spluttered Sellini. 'I don't know who he is or what he is. He met me in a little club in Frith Street and offered me fifty pounds to beat you up. He was a

94

youngish feller, and that's all I know. We was to give you a good beating.'

'And he paid you fifty pounds?' demanded Bellamy.

'He paid me twenty-five down,' answered Sellini, 'and the other twenty-five he was going to give me tomorrow night.'

'At the same place?' asked the bookmaker, and the other nodded. 'What's the name of this place?' said the old man.

'The Green Parrot,' muttered Sellini sullenly. 'And that's all I can tell you, Mr. Bellamy. Now, you let me go.'

'I'll let you go after tomorrer night,' answered the bookmaker calmly. 'Until then you're stayin' 'ere, cock. My housekeeper bought a new clothes line yesterday and there's a good cellar with very little in it but coal. I'm interested in this feller who offered you fifty pounds to beat me up and I think I'll go along to the Green Parrot and collect that other twenty-five he owes you meself, person-ally!'

* * *

Peter Ashton heard the story from Mr. Bellamy's own lips at ten o'clock on the following morning. 'What happened to the fire brigade?' he inquired.

'They're still tryin' to find out who played the trick on them,' Jacob chuckled. 'It was a good stunt, eh?'

'Well,' remarked the reporter, 'it seems as though we might get somewhere if this fellow Sellini is speaking the truth.'

'He's speakin' the truth all right, cock,' said Mr. Bellamy confidently. 'He was too scared to do anything else.'

'And d'you think this man who arranged the beating is connected with the Silver Horseshoe?' asked Peter.

'I'm sure of it. Don't you agree, boy? These people tried to get three thousand quid out of me and failed, and they thought they'd teach me a lesson. We'll be at the Green Parrot tonight and find out just who this feller is.'

Peter frowned. 'I don't think you ought to come,' he remarked. 'If he sees you about the place it may make him suspicious. I'll go; I'm likely to learn more.'

Mr. Bellamy was not at all pleased with this suggestion, but at length he reluctantly agreed. 'All right,' he growled. 'Have it your own way. I suppose you're talkin' sense, really. And anyhow — ' He brightened at the thought. ' — when you've found out who this feller is, I can take a hand again.'

Peter agreed with this, and left him to go to the offices of the *Morning Mail.* Here he discovered that someone had been trying to ring him up, and even while he was attempting to gather information concerning the caller he was told that he was wanted on the phone.

'It's a lady,' said the messenger.

The voice that came over the wire confirmed his hopeful anticipation. It was Marjorie Arbinger. 'I hope you don't mind my ringing you up, Mr. Ashton.' she said. 'But a most peculiar thing has happened. I received a registered packet this morning containing five thousand pounds in notes, and I can't understand who can have sent it or why.'

'Wasn't there anything with it?' asked Peter quickly.

'Nothing,' she answered.

'Extraordinary!' muttered the reporter. 'Where are you phoning from, Miss Arbinger?'

'From home,' she replied.

'May I come and see you?' he went on quickly. 'I'd like to have a look at the envelope.'

'I wish you would,' she answered. 'When will you come?'

'Now!' said Peter promptly. 'I'll be with you just as quickly as I can get there.'

He hung up the instrument and, racing down the stairs, hurried out of the building and round to the side turning where he had parked his little car. Half an hour later he was facing Marjorie Arbinger in the little drawing room at Putney.

'I can't understand it at all!' declared the girl, frowning. 'There's nobody I can think of who could have sent so much money, or any reason why they should. Daddy, so far as I know, had no relations. Anyway, surely there ought to have been a letter enclosed.'

Peter picked up the thick wad of

five-pound notes and examined them. They were crisp and new and had obviously been issued direct from a bank. The wrapping was ordinary: a brown paper parcel with the blue registered label. The postmark showed that the package had been posted on the previous afternoon in the West End of London.

'Queer,' he said, frowning. 'I wonder who could have sent you this?'

'I don't suppose it was Mr. Bellamy?'

'I don't think so,' Peter answered. 'I saw him this morning, and he would have mentioned it. However, it shouldn't be difficult to trace. These notes are new and the bank that issued them will have a record. D'you mind if I take these round to Superintendent Budd? This is really a matter for the police.'

Her faith in the police, since her father's tragic death, was microscopic, but Peter overruled her objections. 'With their organisation,' he pointed out, 'they'll be able to trace this much quicker than we could.'

'Do you think it can have anything to do with the Silver Horseshoe?' she inquired, and he pursed his lips.

'I don't see how it can. But it's mysterious all the same. There must be some reason behind it.'

'What do you think the reason can be?' she asked.

'I haven't the least idea, Miss Arbinger,' Peter declared. 'But I think we ought to try and find out, so I'll take these along to Scotland Yard.'

She consented, and when he told her about Jacob Bellamy's adventure of the previous night and the arrangement they had come to, he took his leave.

Mr. Budd was sprawling in his usual attitude behind his desk when Peter's name was brought in.

'He said he's got important information,' said the messenger.

'They all say that!' grunted the superintendent, whose temper was still a little uncertain. 'But I'll see him. Shoot him up.'

Peter came in cheerily and extended his hand. The stout man lazily raised a fat arm. 'Well now, what's this information you've got?' he demanded.

Peter pulled up a chair and sat down. 'I'll tell you,' he began, and gave a brief account of Marjorie Arbinger's mysterious gift.

Mr. Budd listened, although he gave no appearance that he was even awake. His mouth was slightly open and his eyes completely closed, and his many chins were sunk upon his chest. 'H'm!' he commented, when Peter had finished. 'Interestin' and peculiar. I wish somebody'd send me five thousand pounds. Let's have a look at the wrapping.'

Peter had produced both the notes and the paper in which they had been enclosed, and he pushed these across towards the big man. With a sigh Mr. Budd hoisted himself to a sitting position and looked at them. 'H'm!' he remarked noncommittally. 'And you say the girl has no idea where this came from or why it was sent?'

'None at all!' declared the reporter. 'And I'm a little uneasy about it. That's why I persuaded Miss Arbinger to let me consult you.'

'How do you mean, 'uneasy'?' Mr.

Budd's eyes slowly opened and he surveyed his visitor searchingly.

'Well, it's queer, and I don't like queer things.'

'You must hate my sergeant,' said Mr. Budd, shaking his head. 'He's the queerest thing I've ever come across. Yes, I agree with you, Ashton — it's queer, but I don't see that there's any cause for you to be uneasy.'

'There shouldn't be any difficulty in tracing the notes,' said Peter.

'No,' admitted the other. 'There'll be no difficulty about that, and it'll be interestin' to see where they came from. I'll have it attended to right away.'

'How are you getting on with the Horseshoe business?' asked the reporter.

'To be perfectly candid,' answered Mr. Budd, 'I'm not gettin' on with it. But you don't want to go printin' that in that rag of yours. I don't want no headlines like 'Police completely baffled' and all that sort of stuff. No, I'm not gettin' on with it at all,' he went on. 'That's a queer business, too. There's somethin' behind this that I don't understand at the moment.'

'What makes you think that?' asked Peter curiously.

'Call it a hunch. I've had these hunches before, and they usually turn out right.' Mr. Budd yawned, searched in the pocket of his waistcoat and produced one of his inevitable black cigars. 'When we get to the bottom of this Horseshoe racket,' he continued, 'you'll find I'm right. There's an end to it that we don't know anythin' about.'

Peter was tempted to tell him about the contract which had been made between Jacob Bellamy, the girl, and himself, and the latest developments concerning Tony Sellini; but he refrained, mostly because he realised that his two companions would be averse to taking the police into their confidence.

He took his leave soon after and for some time Mr. Budd sat motionless, his eyes half-closed, trickling little streams of evil-smelling smoke from the corner of his mouth. He was still sitting thus when Leek came in. The lean sergeant caught sight of the pile of money in front of his superior and his eyes widened.

'Hello!' he said. 'How'd you get that?'

'They've just given me a rise,' said Mr. Budd. 'At last my services are bein' properly appreciated.'

'Good lord! There must be quids and quids there!' said Leek. 'Where'd it come from?'

'That feller Ashton brought it,' said Mr. Budd. 'It was sent anonymously to Arbinger's girl this mornin'.' He stretched out a hand and pressed a button on his desk. To the messenger who answered the summons he gave a scribbled note written on an official blank. 'Take that along to Superintendent Yawl,' he murmured, and when the man had gone: 'There's somebody in London givin' away money in large sums, apparently, and I'd like to know who it is.'

'I wish he'd send some to me,' remarked Leek. 'I wouldn't inquire too closely as to where it came from.'

'You wouldn't?' retorted Mr. Budd. 'For a policeman the limitations of your inquirin' mind are remarkable.' He took the stub of his cigar from between his lips and threw it into the fireplace. 'I've got a little job for you,' he said, and Sergeant Leek's melancholy face fell. Mr. Budd's 'little jobs' generally consisted of a great deal of labour which resulted in the most microscopic results, and although they might be useful to the big superintendent they yielded no particular interest to the lean sergeant.

'What d'you want me to do?' he inquired.

'I'll tell you,' said Mr. Budd, and proceeded to do so at some length, to the amazement of his astonished listener.

'What d'you want me to do that for?' he demanded when the superintendent had finished.

'Because I tell you to,' answered Mr. Budd. 'And let's have a little more discipline. How many times have I told you to call me 'sir'?'

'I've lost count,' replied Leek, and hastily added 'sir' as Mr. Budd opened his mouth to utter a further reprimand.

6

The People in the Moonlight

Broad Acres, the ancestral home of the Sevenways, is a considerable estate: with its paddocks, its farms and its flower gardens, it covers a large area of Berkshire and is one of the show places of the district. The house itself dates back to the time when Henry VIII beheaded his first wife; and although during the ensuing years additions and improvements have been added to the original structure, they have been carried out with such care that nothing has been allowed to detract from the beauty of the original building.

On the morning when Peter Ashton had his interview with Mr. Budd at Scotland Yard, Nicolas Melville, ninth Earl of Sevenways, came slowly down the big carved staircase and, as was his invariable habit, stopped in the wide hall to inspect the barometer.

His face was lined and careworn. In truth, Lord Sevenways was undergoing a period of worry that was sapping his small amount of vitality. His financial position was acute, and the mortgage of which he had spoken to John Arbinger was the main cause of his distress. The final day for payment of the interest was drawing rapidly near. The death of the bookmaker had closed the only avenue which had remained open to him to raise the money.

He passed across the big hall and entered the panelled breakfast room. The sun was slanting through the high windows, bringing out the colours of the wood and walls and a bowl of tulips that stood in the centre of the long refectory table. The room was empty, and crossing to one of the windows Sevenways stood staring at the shaven lawn and the gaily hued flowerbeds ablaze with spring blossoms. Away beyond he could see the terrace leading down to the rose garden, as yet giving no hint of the mass of colour which the later months would bring. Beyond that was a coppice of firs leading to the wooded hillside which formed a horseshoe-shaped setting to the house. The beauty of the scene gripped at his heart as it always did, and he sighed as he contemplated the prospect of losing it.

He turned away as the door opened and a footman came in with the morning's mail. 'Good morning, Thomas.'

'Good morning, my lord,' said the man as he arranged the letters he was carrying at the two places set on the long table.

'Her ladyship is not down yet?'

'I haven't seen her, my lord.'

Sevenways strolled over to the table and looked idly at the letters beside his plate. There was one thick registered envelope at which he frowned; the others were evidently bills. He picked up the thick packet and looked at it curiously. It bore a West End postmark and the address was typewritten. Rather puzzled as to what it might contain, he picked up a knife and slid it under the flap. It was a big linen-faced envelope, rather bulky. As he withdrew the contents his frown changed to a look of amazement, for they were bank of England notes, a thick wad of them. He eyed them, unable to believe the evidence of his senses, and then rapidly counted them. Ten thousand pounds! Who in the world could have sent him such a sum?

He searched in the envelope for a letter accompanying this strange gift, but he found nothing. 'Amazing!' he murmured below his breath. 'Where the devil can these have come from?'

The door opened and his wife came in. She was radiant, a fresh and lovely figure in a trim grey costume. 'Good morning, Nicky,' she said cheerily.

'Good morning, my dear,' he answered. 'Do you know anything about this?'

She came to his side and rested a hand affectionately on his shoulder. 'What is it?' she asked, and then, as she saw the notes: 'Where did you get those?'

'I really don't know,' he answered. 'It's most extraordinary, Sybilla! They came by post, in this envelope.'

'But who sent them?' she persisted.

'I don't know. There's no letter with them. Just ten thousand pounds in fifty-pound notes.'

'But somebody must have sent them!' she declared. 'Have you been negotiating for any money?'

'I've been trying to raise sufficient to pay that infernal interest,' he answered. 'But when John Arbinger was killed my last hope went. It's deuced extraordinary! I haven't the faintest idea where these could have come from.'

'Well, don't let's look a gift horse in the mouth,' she said gaily. 'What's the interest, six thousand? That leaves four thousand in hand.'

'But my dear girl,' he protested, 'I can't use this money unless I know where it's come from! There must be some mistake.'

'The mistake is on the part of the sender,' said Lady Sevenways firmly, and then: 'Don't you realise what it means, Nicky? You can save Broad Acres and the horses.'

Her husband, still rather dazed, nodded. 'Yes. Yes, my dear, I suppose I can,' he murmured.

'Perhaps you have an unknown friend who has heard of your difficulty,' said Sybilla. 'Don't worry, Nicky. You've got the money, and it's good money — at least I suppose it is.'

This idea had not occurred to his lordship, and he fingered one of the notes cautiously. 'It seems all right to me,' he answered. 'But where the devil can it have come from?'

'It's a gift from the gods,' said his wife, smiling. 'You'll be able to send a cheque to Mortons today, and another to Ledgers. You won't have to send the horses to Tattersalls after all.'

Sevenways's brow cleared. The thought of having to sell his racers had worried him almost more than the possibility of losing his beloved Broad Acres. 'Well, I suppose there's something in that, my dear,' he remarked. 'Anyway, I'll pay them into the bank after breakfast.'

He thrust the notes into his pocket as the butler came in with several covered dishes. When the meal was over he made an excuse to his wife and retired to his study, and here he spent a considerable time telephoning various friends and business acquaintances to try and trace the source of the unexpected gift. But he found no clue. Although he tried everyone he could think of, none of them, including his solicitors, seemed to know anything about the mysterious ten thousand pounds.

He gave it up at last and ordering the car, was driven to his bank where he paid in the amount, causing no little astonishment to Mr. Leslie, the manager. It was some considerable time since Lord Sevenways had handled such a large sum.

In the afternoon he sent off the cheque to Morton's and held a telephone conversation with his trainer, informing him, to that man's unconcealed delight, that there was no longer any need to dispose of the string of thoroughbred racers.

'I galloped Barley Sugar this morning, my lord,' said the trainer, 'and it's my opinion we've got a real find.'

'I'll come down and see you tomorrow,' said Sevenways, and rang off.

The peculiar gift worried and unsettled him. He was a little nervous, too, that there might be something wrong with the money against which he had already drawn two considerable cheques. Supposing it was a mistake? Supposing someone had put it in the wrong envelope and it had reached him by accident and they claimed it back?

He suggested this to his wife at dinner, but she refused to be pessimistic. 'Wait till they do, Nicky,' she said. 'Then you can worry. At the present moment we're out of all our troubles, so why not accept the fact and stop bothering?' She looked across at him affectionately. 'You've been looking very peaky lately,' she went on, 'and I know it's been money that's worrying you. Now forget it.'

He tried to follow her advice, but it was not so easy. Throughout the rest of the evening he still continued to puzzle his brain, and even after they had parted for the night and he had sought his room the extraordinary gift from the clouds kept him wakeful.

It must have been one o'clock when he heard the footfall. It came stealthily past his door, a soft creak, and he sat up in bed listening intently. Then he heard the creak of a stair and knew that he had not imagined it. Perhaps one of the servants was ill.

He got up quickly, pulled on a dressing gown, and thrust his feet into his slippers. Going over to the door, he opened it. There was no sound in the silent house except the soft ticking of the big grandfather clock below. Then he heard the rattle of a bolt and the tinkle of a chain. Someone was letting themselves out by the main door.

He went swiftly along the corridor, paused at the head of the stairs, and leaned over the balustrade. It was dark below and he could see nothing, but a wind came up to him which told him that the front door was open. Curious to discover who was going out at such an hour, he went quickly down the stairs, crossed the hall and paused on the top of the steps, looking out into the moonlit night. But whoever had left the house was now out of sight. He could see no one.

The mysterious gift of money, coupled with this night's activity on the part of some member of his household, disturbed him.

He moved aimlessly down the steps onto the broad gravel of the drive, peering in all directions. But nothing stirred in the immediate vicinity. He reached the lawn, rounded a clump of shrubbery, and came to a sudden stop with a queer, sick feeling in the pit of his stomach.

Near the big acacia tree that stood in the centre of the smaller lawn, clearly outlined in the moonlight, stood his wife. She was talking to a man, a stranger. They were standing very close together, obviously quite unaware that there was an eavesdropper.

So it was Sybilla who had crept furtively out of the house at that late hour, to meet — whom?

He watched, his mouth dry, his eyes straining. His wife was speaking rapidly, accompanying her words with little gestures, oddly familiar gestures that she used when she was excited. And the man was listening, interpolating a word here and there. Presently he passed something to the woman and she slipped it into the bosom of her dress. It was only then that Sevenways noticed that she was still wearing the gown she had worn at dinner.

This meeting then had been prear-
ranged. She had not undressed. His eyes
felt suddenly surprisingly hot and wet,
and he gripped his lower lip between his
teeth. Sybilla!

It had never entered his head to suspect
that she was deceiving him over anything,
and now . . . He shook himself angrily.
Perhaps, after all, there was nothing in it.
Maybe there was some explanation for
this meeting which he had witnessed.
Perhaps she was in some kind of trouble.
He knew very little about his wife before
he met her. Possibly this man was trying
to blackmail her. He had read of such
things. In which event, of course, she
could count on him.

And then, even as the thought came to
him, he saw how absurd it had been, for
the man had moved nearer, slipped his
arm round the woman's shoulders, and
drawn her to him. As they kissed, Lord
Sevenways turned away and went stumbling blindly back towards the house.

★ ★ ★

A little more than two-thirds of the way down Frith Street on the right-hand side is a dark and narrow doorway, distinguished from all the other dark and narrow doorways in its immediate vicinity by the greenly glittering outline of a parrot in neon tubes which shines brilliantly over the facia from dusk until the early hours. Beyond the doorway lies a dimly lighted passage, terminating in another door covered with green baize. Beyond this second door is a small vestibule with a blank wall on one side and a narrow counter on the other, behind which a sleepy-eyed gentleman in rather shabby evening clothes presides over a rack of hats and overcoats.

He is in charge also of a greasy-looking book in which, should you have ventured so far, you would be required to sign your name and pay a fee before being allowed to sample the amenities of the Green Parrot Club, the raucous sounds of which can be heard faintly through the double doors at the other end of the vestibule. If there is any reason to suspect your credentials you will receive a sad shake of

117

the head and a reminder that only members are admitted, and that unless you can produce your membership card you had best give up all hope of entering the holy of holies beyond.

How the Green Parrot avoided being struck off the register and closed for good was a mystery to everyone concerned except its polyglot proprietor. He knew, but kept the information to himself, for his clients would not have appreciated the true explanation, which was simple in the extreme. The police were perfectly aware of the nefarious clientele which gathered nightly to drink and dance in the smoke-filled room which had once been a mission hall, but they allowed certain latitudes on the part of Mr. Solly Zinnerman; not, however, without receiving a *quid pro quo* for these considerations. So long as nothing really flagrant took place on the premises they were prepared to close their eyes to such mild law-breaking as drinking after hours, for the place was useful in more ways than one.

It was the nightly rendezvous of half

the habitual criminals in the Soho district, and occasionally from farther afield, and a 'wanted' man could generally be found there sooner or later. Many were the useful items of information which Mr. Zinnerman had been able to pass on to the proper quarter, although this was unknown to the customers who honoured him with their patronage. Had it been thought that the stout little proprietor had been responsible for the arrest of a number of his clientele, he would not have remained long in a position to run a club or anything else — he would have passed swiftly and violently to, it is hoped, a better land.

Peter Ashton arrived at the Green Parrot at a little after eleven, and it was not his first visit by any means. The cloakroom attendant-cum-reception-clerk greeted him with the friendly smile that he reserved for such customers as were welcome, and Peter, handing over his hat and coat, scrawled his signature beneath a line of others that were more or less illegible.

'Busy tonight, Tich?' he inquired.

119

'Fairly,' answered the little man behind the counter. 'But it's early yet. We don' really fill up till about one.'

'Any of the Sellini boys here?' asked the reporter.

Tich pursed his lips. 'Now you're asking something, Mister Ashton,' he said. 'You know the motter 'ere: 'Ask no questions and you won't 'ear no lies'.' He winked, and Peter grinned.

'OK,' he said. 'I get you.' He slipped a ten-shilling note across the counter and waved away the change. 'Buy yourself a drink, Tich, when you get a chance,' he said, and passed on into the main portion of the building.

A burst of tinny music greeted his ears as he pushed open the double doors, and pausing on the shallow steps that led down to the dance floor he surveyed the scene before him. The room was long and narrow, and decorated in green and white. At the opposite end was a raised dais on which stood a piano, a trap-drum, and four black bandsmen dressed in dingy green uniforms. The lights were dim, and rendered dimmer by the parrot-shaped shades of green silk that covered the naked bulbs and the blue haze of tobacco smoke that hung heavily in the scented air.

The atmosphere was fetid, a combination of tobacco and cheap perfume. Round the small polished floor on which half a dozen couples were shuffling up and down to the frenzied efforts of the band were a number of glass-topped tables and basket chairs. At these sat a miscellaneous collection of humanity, some in evening dress, some in ordinary lounge suits, and representing almost every breed and cross-breed. There were flashily dressed girls with brassy hair, over made-up and haggard beneath the paint, whose weary eyes held in their depths a calculating hardness. It was a cosmopolitan gathering of which nearly every person was a human cocktail, so marked was the mixture of blood. There were every conceivable mixture of races. As Peter stood eyeing the familiar scene a fat little man with a large, wobbling paunch came forward out of the dimness and approached him.

'Good evening, Mister Ashton,' said Solly Zinnerman. 'It's a long time since we've had the pleasure of entertaining you, eh?'

'Quite a while,' murmured Peter. 'How are things, Solly?'

'Not so bad,' he lisped. 'One or two of my best clients are away on holiday. Not so bad.'

Peter grinned to himself. 'On holiday' meant at the Government's expense, and was the euphemism employed by the underworld to signify a 'stretch'.

'What brings you here tonight, Mr. Ashton?' went on Zinnerman, eyeing him keenly. 'Local colour, eh?'

'That's it,' said Peter. 'I've come to see how the poor live.'

Mr. Zinnerman's stomach wobbled up and down as he chuckled. 'The poor don't come here, Mr. Ashton,' he said.

'Seen Tony Sellini lately?' asked the reporter, and the other nodded.

'He was here when — last evening? No. The evening before. He did not come in last evening. He will be here tonight, later perhaps.'

Will he? thought Peter grimly. *I think it's very doubtful, my friend.* 'Any of the boys here?' he asked aloud.

'Yes, one or two,' Mr. Zinnerman replied. 'They come and go. You know how it is.'

'I'll go and find a table,' Peter said. 'See you later, Solly.'

There were plenty of spare tables, for the night was young according to the habits of the patrons of the Green Parrot; and selecting one from which he could obtain a view of the entire room, he pulled out a chair and sat down. A tired waiter came up and Peter ordered a whisky and soda. When it was brought to him he lit a cigarette and, leaning back in his chair, took a more detailed stock of his surroundings.

Several of the Sellini gang he knew by sight, and he picked out two who were sitting at a table almost opposite to him, talking rapidly in low tones. The man on account of whom he had come to the place might have been one of many, for the description which old Jacob Bellamy had succeeded in forcing out of Tony

Sellini was sketchy. His only means of really judging his quarry would be from his behaviour. He would naturally be expecting Sellini, and would probably, therefore, be on the alert for his arrival.

He selected three likely-looking people and watched them covertly, but none of them appeared as if they were awaiting the arrival of anybody. His eyes presently lighted on a man who was sitting by himself at a table in a corner, and who hardly looked in keeping with the rest of the crowd that frequented the Green Parrot. He was a little jovial-faced man with large horn-rimmed glasses, attired in immaculate evening dress. Before him stood a tall glass of some yellow liquid which Peter concluded was whisky and soda, and from which he occasionally took an appreciative sip.

American, thought the reporter. *Now what's his graft?* He became aware, to his surprise, that the other was watching him with an equal interest. To his knowledge he had never seen the jovial-faced individual before. Why, therefore, was the man paying him so much attention?

The band stopped in the middle of a particularly untuneful din, and there was a little outburst of clapping from the dancers. After a moment's pause the band broke into fresh and equally unmelodious noise, and as the couples once more became animated by the rhythm Peter saw the stout little man rise slowly to his feet and begin to make his way towards the table at which he was sitting.

'I guess you're Mr. Ashton,' he greeted in a pleasant voice, which confirmed Peter's supposition of his country of origin.

'I guess the same,' said Peter. 'Has my fame crossed the Atlantic?'

'No, sir!' answered the man who called himself 'Superstitious Sam'. 'But you were pointed out to me the other day and I thought I hadn't made a mistake.'

'Such is notoriety,' said Peter. 'Suppose we finish the introduction properly?'

'My name's Piggott,' said the other, taking the hint. 'Samuel K. Piggott at your service, sir.'

'I'm very pleased to meet you, Mr. Piggott,' said Peter. 'Are you over here on holiday or on business?'

'On business, sir,' was the reply. 'I'm fifty-two this coming August and I haven't had a holiday since I left school.'

'You must be getting pretty tired,' remarked the reporter. 'Sit down and have a drink.' He snapped his fingers to attract the attention of a passing waiter.

Mr. Piggott bowed his thanks, pulled out a chair, and dropped gently into it. 'I'll have a highball — or, as you call them over here, a whisky and soda,' said Mr. Piggott.

Peter gave the order and waited, his curiosity aroused, to see what was coming next. He was prepared for almost anything except his companion's next remark.

'Maybe he won't come,' he murmured.

Peter started. 'Who won't come?'

'The fellow you're waiting for,' answered Mr. Piggott; and his eyes, behind the big spectacles, met the reporter's astonished gaze solemnly.

'How do you know I'm waiting for anybody?' said Peter.

'Call it a guess,' replied 'Superstitious

Sam', 'and then tell me if I'm wrong.'
When the reporter made no reply he
added: 'Well, perhaps it isn't necessary to
tell me. I guess I'm not wrong.'

'You seem fond of guesses!' retorted
Peter, and the other chuckled.

'Yes, sir, I am,' he answered. 'You'd be
surprised at some of the things I've been
guessing lately. Here's one of my guesses.
I guess the fellow you're waiting for
knows Tony Sellini ain't able to come
here tonight and won't turn up either.' He
smiled complacently.

Peter eyed him curiously. 'You seem to
know a great deal,' he remarked. 'Perhaps
you can tell me who this man is I'm
supposed to be waiting for?'

'Perhaps I can,' agreed Mr. Piggott. He
leaned across the table confidentially. 'You're
a friend of Superintendent Budd's, aren't
you? Well, I'll pass on the warning to you
that I gave to him. Be careful! Horseshoes
can be dangerous things. Particularly silver
ones. Get me?'

'I get you,' said Peter, his eyes
narrowing. 'What do you know about the
Silver Horseshoe?'

'Very little,' said Mr. Piggott. 'But I guess a lot. The man you're waiting for tonight is dangerous, and he won't come.'

'Do you know him?' said the reporter quickly, and the round, jovial face before him moved up and down in an affirmative nod.

'Yes, I know him,' answered Mr. Piggott slowly. 'P'raps one day I'll introduce you, but it won't be yet.'

7

Mr. Mervyn Holt, Solicitor

Mr. Budd raised his head and slowly opened his eyes as there came a tap on the door of his office. 'Come in,' he grunted huskily, and a stockily built man entered. 'Mornin', Rush,' said the big man. 'Well, any luck?'

Detective Sergeant Rush nodded. 'Yes, sir,' he answered. 'I've succeeded in tracing those notes. They were issued through the account of a Mr. Mervyn Holt, solicitor.'

The stout superintendent hoisted himself to a sitting position and pulled a note-block towards him. 'What's this feller's address?' he asked.

Rush produced a black-covered book, turned over the pages, and consulted some notes. 'Ashley Chambers, Lynchford Street, Bloomsbury,' he read aloud.

Mr. Budd noted it down. 'And you say

the notes were issued through his bank?' he grunted.

'That's right,' said Rush. 'The Kingsway branch of the Northern and Midland. This man Holt drew a cheque to self and cashed it personally, receiving notes in exchange.'

'Must be pretty well off to be able to do that. Five thousand pounds is a lot of money.'

'The money was paid into his account two days before the cheque was issued,' explained Rush, his eyes on the pages of the black book. 'It was paid in pound notes which, the manager of the bank informs me, are untraceable.'

'In pound notes, eh?' The big man pursed his lips and scratched the lowest of his many chins. 'Queer! He has five thousand paid in and he draws the five thousand out and sends it to Miss Arbinger, or somebody does. Very queer! And these Silver Horseshoe people, in their demands, stipulated pound notes.'

'Is this business connected with the Silver Horseshoe, sir?' asked Rush, who had not been informed as to the reason for his inquiries.

'I don't know,' said the big man, 'but it seems likely. All right, Rush, you've done very well. I think I'll have a word with this feller Mervyn Holt myself.'

He sat for some time lost in thought after the sergeant had departed, and then rising slowly and laboriously to his feet he put on his hat and left the office. He passed out of Scotland Yard and boarded a bus that would take him to Bloomsbury.

Lynchford Street proved to be a narrow cul-de-sac, and Ashley Chambers was an old and dirty block of offices on the right-hand side near the end. Mr. Budd inspected the uninviting entrance dubiously. Not at all the type of place where he would have expected to find a prosperous solicitor. Perhaps Mr. Mervyn Holt wasn't prosperous. Quite obviously this money had not been his own. The question was for whom was he acting, and it was a question that the stout superintendent thought might prove difficult to answer.

He entered the narrow doorway and

ascended the twisting stone staircase beyond. On the third landing he came upon a door bearing in black letters the inscription:

MERVYN HOLT. SOLICITOR.
INQUIRIES.

Pushing open the door, he went in and found himself in a dark and narrow passage-like apartment, across one end of which ran a mahogany counter. A pimply-faced youth was sitting at a dusty and littered table, typing furiously. He looked up as Mr. Budd came to a halt by the counter, rose, and approached him.

'Yes, sir?' he said inquiringly.

'Mr. Holt in?' murmured the big man. 'I'd like to see him.'

'If you'll give me your name I'll see if Mr. Holt is disengaged,' said the youth.

The stout superintendent plunged a hand into his pocket and produced a card which he passed across the counter. The pimply-faced clerk took it, glanced at the name, saw his visitor's rank and the address New Scotland Yard, and his jaw dropped. His eyes were scared as he surveyed the other.

'If — if you'll wait, I'll go and see.' He disappeared through a door in the wall and Mr. Budd heard the murmur of voices. The youth was absent some time. Evidently Mr. Mervyn Holt was not eager to receive his visitor, and from this evident reluctance the big man deduced that all was not as it should be with Mr. Holt.

After nearly five minutes the clerk reappeared. 'Mr. Holt will see you,' he announced. 'This way, please.' He lifted a flap in the counter and Mr. Budd squeezed himself through. Conducting him over to the door, the still scared-looking clerk ushered him into an inner office — a small, poky room, very dusty and dirty, and occupied by a very large man at a very large desk, who surveyed him between two enormous piles of dust-covered documents carefully tied with red tape.

'Er — Superintendent Budd?' inquired a throaty, guttural voice, and Mr. Budd nodded.

'You Mr. Holt, sir?' he inquired in his turn.

'Yes,' said the large man, 'I am Mervyn Holt. What can I do for you?'

The superintendent looked round for a chair and discovered a dilapidated leather-covered one. Pulling it forward, he sat down. For a moment he took stock of the man before him in silence, and he was not impressed by what he saw. Mr. Holt's large face was grey and unhealthy-looking, his head covered thinly with curly black hair that shone brilliantly in the light that percolated through the dirty panes of a window behind him. His soft, fat hands that were nervously rolling a pencil up and down the blotting pad were covered with large orange-coloured freckles, and the cuffs of his shirt, which projected over his wrists, were frayed.

'I've called to inquire,' began Mr. Budd slowly, 'into a little matter concerning five thousand pounds that was sent to a Miss Arbinger. I think you know something about it.'

An expression of relief crossed the strained face of the lawyer. 'Oh,' he said throatily, 'that's it, is it? Well, I don't know whether I'm — er — justified in giving you any information.'

'I understand,' went on Mr. Budd, ignoring the fact of whether he was justified or not, 'that these notes were sent by you.'

Mr. Holt nodded slowly. 'I see no reason for disguising the fact,' he remarked ponderously. 'Yes, those notes were sent by me to Miss Arbinger.'

'I should like to know for what reason,' said the stout man, and Mr. Holt shook his head.

'I'm afraid I cannot divulge the reason,' he said. 'The transaction was a confidential one between myself and my — er — client, and therefore I am not at liberty to discuss it.'

Mr. Budd had expected something like this and was not surprised. 'You'll understand, sir,' he said heavily, 'that Miss Arbinger was naturally rather astonished to receive such a large sum anonymously and, quite naturally, consulted the police. We put through inquiries and discovered that these notes had been drawn by you from your account at the Northern and Midland Bank, and therefore since there seems to be some mystery attached to the sending of the money to Miss Arbinger, we hoped you would be in a position to clear it up.'

'I regret,' said Mr. Holt, 'that I cannot help you. My client, whose name I am not in a position to divulge, instructed me to forward this money to Miss Arbinger. And I carried out these instructions. That is as far as I am concerned with the matter.'

'You are, of course,' said Mr. Budd, 'aware of the identity of your client?'

'Oh, yes. I am quite aware of the identity of my client.'

'But,' continued the superintendent, 'you refuse to divulge it. Is that it?'

'That is it sir,' said Mr. Holt. 'And, as you will agree with me, I am legally entitled not to. It is not a criminal offence for one person to send money to another person anonymously, so long as that money has been acquired honestly. You agree with me?'

'I agree with you up to a point,' said

Mr. Budd seriously. 'This money which you drew out of your account and sent to Miss Arbinger was covered by an equal sum paid into your account in pound notes. This, I presume, was given you by your client?'

'That is correct,' said the lawyer.

'But,' continued the superintendent, 'how can you be certain that this money was obtained by your client honestly? It's a peculiar thing for such a large sum to be in pound notes. There's only one possible explanation, and that is because pound notes are untraceable.'

'I can assure you, sir,' said Mr. Holt with dignity, 'that my client is a person above suspicion. His explanation for the money being paid into my account in pound notes is a simple one. My client and I were expecting that some effort would be made on the part of Miss Arbinger to trace the origin of this money, and therefore precautions were taken to avoid any such endeavour being successful. It was immaterial — ' He waved a podgy hand. ' — whether the notes sent to Miss Arbinger should be traced to me; that I did not mind. But it was essential, according to my client's views, that my client should remain anonymous. That is the explanation as to why the money was paid into my account in pound notes.'

It was a plausible explanation, and Mr. Budd found himself in a quandary. He had no legal right to press his inquiries, and obviously Mr. Mervyn Holt knew this. Nothing of a criminal nature could be proved in the mysterious transaction, and therefore it was not a job for the police.

'Then that is all the information you are prepared to give?'

'Certainly,' said Mr. Holt. 'I'm sorry, Superintendent, but in the circumstances my duty to my client prohibits any confidences. In the event, of course, of you being able to assure me that, from the legal standpoint, I am wrong, I am prepared to reconsider my decision.'

Since the stout man could not do this, he thanked the lawyer and took his leave. He was by no means satisfied. The whole situation was, to use his own favourite expression, 'interestin' and peculiar'. People do not as a rule send other people large sums of money anonymously without a very good reason. What was the reason in the case of Marjorie Arbinger, and who was the mysterious donor of the gift? Why, too, had this person chosen Mervyn Holt? Anyone in command of a large sum like five thousand pounds would reasonably be expected to have their own solicitor, and they certainly would not choose such a person as the man he had just interviewed.

Mr. Budd was experienced enough to guess that all was not so open and above-board with Mr. Mervyn Holt as that gentleman tried to make out. His business, from the appearance of his office, was not a flourishing one. It was all very queer, and it occupied his mind to the exclusion of all else as he was carried back to Scotland Yard.

Turning in at the Whitehall entrance, he came to a decision. Mr. Mervyn Holt would be worth inquiring into, and the first thing he did when he reached his office was to put such inquiries in motion.

* * *

Peter Ashton reported his failure to Jacob Bellamy on the morning following his wasted evening at the Green Parrot, and received an invitation from the old man to come and talk things over at his house that night. It was seven o'clock when Peter arrived, and he was admitted by the bookmaker himself, who led the way into his study and splashed whisky into two glasses with a prodigal hand.

''ere, get that inside you,' he said, 'and then tell me all about it.'

Peter swallowed a mouthful of the drink and then did so. Jacob Bellamy listened interestedly.

'I'd like to know more about this feller Piggott,' he said. 'He seems to know a lot, don't he?'

'He knows a great deal too much, in my opinion,' said Peter. 'I can't place him at all. He's an American, but he doesn't look like a crook to me. Yet he certainly knew this fellow wasn't turning up.'

'Maybe it was a gag,' suggested Jacob. 'Maybe the feller was there all the time and this chap was just tryin' to cover 'im. Get what I mean?'

'Yes, I get what you mean,' said Peter. 'But I don't think you're right. I kept my eyes skinned all the while, and I saw nobody who looked as if he might be the man we're after.'

'H'm. Well, it wasn't entirely a wasted evenin'. We've discovered a man who *does* know somethin',' explained old Jacob, pointing his remark by waving his glass. 'This man Piggott. We've got to keep in touch with him because he might lead us to the people we want.'

'Well he's easy enough to find,' said Peter. 'He lives at the Gresham Hotel, Norfolk Street.'

'What, did he tell you his address?' Jacob asked.

'No. But I left before he did,' Peter explained, 'and waited for him to come out. He took a taxi and I followed in another, and that's where he went to. He's staying in his own name, too. I inquired of the night porter. What are you going to do with Sellini?'

'I was wonderin' that meself, cock,' said Jacob with a grin, swallowing the remainder of his drink and setting down the empty glass.

'Perhaps he hasn't told us all he knows,' suggested the reporter.

'I think he has,' said the bookmaker. 'Anyhow, we can have him up if you'd like to see him.'

He left the room and after a slight delay returned, holding by the arm a weird object that had once been the flashily dressed and immaculate Tony Sellini. The man was covered from head to foot in coal dust, and presented a ludicrous spectacle.

''ere 'e is,' grunted Jacob, pushing his captive into a chair. 'Nice lookin' specimen, ain't 'e?'

''ow much longer are you goin' to keep me shut up in that there cellar?' whined Sellini. 'It ain't right! I could 'ave the law on you.'

'You couldn't have anythin' on me!' snarled Jacob. 'Listen here, Sellini. You've been tellin' lies. That feller you spoke about never turned up.'

'That ain't my fault,' answered Sellini. 'What I told you is the truth, Mr. Bellamy. S'elp me 'tis. If 'e didn't turn up it was because 'e knew I couldn't get there.'

'How could he have known that?' demanded Peter.

'I dunno,' said the gang leader. 'P'raps he was watching when we tried to beat up Mr. Bellamy.'

'Well, what I want to know,' said Jacob, 'is who he is. Now come on, Sellini — out with it. You haven't told all you know.'

'I swear I 'ave. I dunno who the fellow is. I never set eyes on 'im before in my life until that night 'e came to the Green Parrot and offered me fifty quid to beat you up. That's as true as I'm sittin' 'ere!'

He stuck to that statement in spite of both Peter's and Bellamy's endeavours, and they were forced to believe that he was speaking the truth.

'Well, what are we goin' to do with 'im?' asked the bookmaker, looking at Peter.

'I suggest,' said Peter, 'that you turn him over to the police.'

'If you do that,' broke in the prisoner, 'you'll have to explain what you meant by keepin' me locked up in that cellar!'

'I've got an idea, cock,' said Jacob suddenly. 'Come 'ere, you.' He yanked the expostulating Sellini up by the collar of his coat and propelled him towards the door. 'I'll be back in a minute, boy,' he said over his shoulder, and disappeared. Presently he returned. 'I've just shut 'im up again for a bit,' he said. 'Now listen — we'll keep him till later on this evenin' and then I'll turn 'im loose. You can follow 'im. I bet 'e goes straight to the Green Parrot after 'e's 'ad a wash and spruced 'imself up a little to try and collect the balance of 'is fifty quid. And you can follow 'im. That's what we ought to 'ave done in the first place.'

Peter was dubious. 'It might have worked then, but I doubt if it will now. There's something in what he said about this man, whoever he is, being aware of what happened. That's probably why he didn't turn up last night.'

144

'If he didn't,' said Mr. Bellamy. 'Anyhow, it's worth tryin', cock. Are you game?'

'Oh, I'm game for anything that'll give us a lead to these people. My news editor is getting impatient at the lack of sensation, and — '

A sharp rat-tat from the hall broke into his sentence and he looked inquiringly at the bookmaker.

'Postman, cock,' said Jacob laconically. "alf a tick.'

He went out, returning with a letter which he ripped open. His face changed as he read the contents, and then he tossed the single sheet over to his friend. 'Take a look at that!' he growled, and Peter obeyed.

The sheet of common typing paper bore neither date nor other heading, and the letter began abruptly:

'*You have been lucky up to the present, but your luck will not hold forever. You have defied us and therefore you must pay the penalty. Between now and Friday the sixteenth you will pay the sum of five*

145

thousand pounds in pound notes and in the manner stipulated below.

'On Thursday you will be attending the race meeting at Gatwick in the usual course of your business. To a man who will present you with a card bearing the insignia of the Silver Horseshoe you will hand over the sum mentioned. If any attempt is made to evade this liability, invoke the aid of the police, or detain the messenger, you will be killed within an hour of any such disobedience of these orders.'

Below the line of typing was the stamped impression of a silver horseshoe.

'What d'you think of that?' demanded Jacob when Peter had finished reading.

'I think,' said the reporter seriously, 'they mean business. I shouldn't treat this lightly, Jacob, if I were you.'

'They're not gettin' any five thousand quid outer me!' said the bookmaker decisively. 'But it gives us another chance. If we're clever we might pinch the lot this time.'

8

Mr. Budd Is Annoyed

Peter had opened his mouth to reply when they were startled by a thunderous tattoo on the front door knocker. 'Who the heck can that be?' grunted Jacob.

The reporter got up quickly. 'I'll go,' he said. 'It might be trouble.'

He went out into the hall, crossed to the front door, and after a second's hesitation jerked back the catch and pulled it open. A bulky figure stood on the steps, silhouetted against the fading light of the ending day. It was Mr. Budd.

'Oh, hel — hello!' In his surprise Peter stammered slightly. 'What are you doing here?'

The big man eyed him sleepily. 'I wanted to see you,' he replied heavily. 'I've been chasin' you about for a long time, and your paper told me I'd probably find you here.'

Peter remembered having mentioned his intention of visiting Jacob Bellamy to Mr. Sorbet. 'Well, here I am,' he said.

'Got one or two things I want to talk to you about,' murmured Mr. Budd. 'Shall I come in or will you come out?'

'Come in.' Peter held the door wider. 'You know Jacob Bellamy, don't you?'

The superintendent nodded as he stepped ponderously into the hall. 'The bookmaker,' he said. 'Yes, I know him.'

The bookmaker himself appeared at that moment at the open door of his study. 'Who is it, boy?' he called.

'One of the big four from Scotland Yard,' replied Peter, with a grin. 'In fact, the biggest of the lot.'

The old man came quickly towards them, recognised Mr. Budd, and held out a huge hand. 'Long time since I seen you, cock,' he grunted. 'Not since the old days at 'Basham' Martin's, eh? Come in and have a drink.' He led the way into the lighted study, indicated a chair, and turned to a tray on a side table. 'What'll you have, whisky?' he asked.

'I'd rather have beer,' Mr. Budd

answered slowly. 'Beer's a good, whole-some drink.'

'But fattening,' put in Peter.

'Well, maybe,' said the stout man. 'But a bit o' fat never did anyone any harm.'

'Beer you shall have,' said Bellamy. ''alf a tick.'

He left the room, and Peter shot a quick glance at the reclining detective. 'Well, what do you want with me?' he asked.

'Quite a lot of things,' said Mr. Budd. 'You was at the Green Parrot last night, wasn't yer?'

'How did you know that?' demanded the reporter.

'Never mind how I know,' said the big man impatiently. 'I do know, and that's all that matters. And you was talkin' to a feller called Piggott,' continued the superintendent. 'You was talkin' to him for the best part of the evenin', and when he left you followed him.'

'You're certainly a mine of informa-tion,' remarked Peter. 'How do you know all this? Are you having me trailed?'

'No,' Mr. Budd answered. 'But I'm

havin' Piggott trailed. And the man who was trailin' him reported that he'd met you.'

'Oh, I see. Who is this man Piggott?'

'That I can't tell you,' said Mr. Budd. 'He's an American, which I expect you've guessed for yourself. And he came over two months ago on the *Eureka*. But apart from that I don't know nothin' about him. I'd like to,' he added.

'Well, you are in much the same position as I am,' said Peter.

'That's a pity,' Mr. Budd said. 'I was hopin' that maybe you'd be able to tell me somethin' about Mr. Samuel K. Piggott.'

'Is that what you came here for?' asked the reporter.

'Partly,' said Mr. Budd. 'Partly — ' He broke off as old Jacob came back with an inviting-looking tankard.

'Here y'are, cock. That's the best drop of beer you've ever tasted, I'll bet.'

Mr. Budd took the tankard and sampled the contents. 'Not so bad,' he remarked, smacking his lips. 'Yes, it's a good drop of beer, Mr. Bellamy.' He took a long pull and settled back in his chair once more, resting the tankard on his broad knee. 'What was you doin' at the Green Parrot?' he inquired suddenly.

'I just dropped in.' Peter was vague.

'I see.' Mr. Budd surveyed him through half-closed eyes. 'You just dropped in, met this man Piggott, and then just dropped out again?'

'That's right,' said the reporter.

The superintendent grunted. 'Were you hurt the other evenin', Mr. Bellamy?'

'Hurt?' Jacob swung round, a whisky bottle in one hand and a glass in the other.

'I'm talkin' about the Sellini lot. They tried to beat you up, but luckily somebody broke a fire alarm and they cleared off.'

'Oh, that!' Bellamy dismissed the matter as though it was of no account. 'I'd almost forgotten. No, I wasn't hurt.'

'Very lucky indeed,' said Mr. Budd. 'What happened to Sellini? Was he hurt?'

'Sellini?' repeated the old man. 'I don't know nothin' about Sellini.'

'Queer.' Mr. Budd gently twirled the tankard and eyed it thoughtfully. 'Nobody's seen Sellini since that night. Even his own gang don't know what happened to him. I was wonderin' whether perhaps you was lookin' for him at the Green Parrot, Mr. Ashton.'

Peter exchanged a quick look with Bellamy. 'Why should I be looking for him?' he asked.

'The Green Parrot's one of his favourite haunts. You was there, and now I find you talkin' to Mr. Bellamy, and Mr. Bellamy was attacked by Sellini's gang. What was the idea?' He looked towards the bookmaker and Jacob took a gulp of the fresh drink he had poured out.

'I suppose I must 'ave done somethin' to offend 'em,' he grunted. 'It's not unusual for a race gang to attack a bookmaker.'

'It's unusual for them to attack him so far away from their own territory,' said the detective. 'So you don't know why they wanted to beat you up? You don't know what's happened to Sellini?'

'Why should I know what's happened to a greasy little swine?'

'I suppose there's no reason, really,' said Mr. Budd. He took a long drink of beer and then, suddenly: 'Why didn't you report the fact that you'd had a Silver Horseshoe letter to the police?'

The sudden question startled both the bookmaker and Peter. 'How did you know I had a — a Silver Horseshoe letter?' asked the old man.

Mr. Budd sat up and set the empty tankard carefully down on the floor beside his chair. 'I didn't know,' he said. 'But I know now. I thought maybe you had when they told me Mr. Ashton had come to see you. It was just a question of puttin' two and two together and makin' four. Suppose you tell me all about it?'

Bellamy hesitated. He was not best pleased at the trap into which he had fallen. This slow-looking sleepy-eyed man had stampeded him into an admission which he had had no intention of making. Peter saw his hesitation and intervened.

'I suppose we might as well tell him, Jacob,' he said. 'After all, there's no knowing that he mightn't be useful.'

'Thanks,' said Mr. Budd. 'I take that as a compliment, Mr. Ashton.'

'Oh, well, tell him if you want to,' Jacob

growled. 'Though I'm not goin' to alter my original intention of fightin' these people meself.'

'So that was the idea, was it?' murmured the big man. 'A sort of little private police force of your own, eh?'

'Well, the official force didn't seem to be doin' much!' snapped the old man.

'The official force,' said Mr. Budd, 'are doin' all they can. And they could do more if people'd only come forward and give 'em all the information at their disposal. Now, I think you'd be wise to tell me all you know.' There was an edge to his voice which had not been there before.

Peter told him everything, and the fat man listened in silence.

'I wish you'd come to me in the first place,' he remarked as the reporter concluded. 'You've done more harm than good. If you'd come to me we might have been able to do somethin'. As it is, it's too late.'

'We thought — ' began Peter.

'I know what you thought,' broke in Mr, Budd irritably. 'You thought what a great many people have thought before.

You thought that the three of you were so darned clever that you could do more than what the police could do! And you've only succeeded in doin' nothin'! Let me tell you this.' He leaned forward, tapping his knee. 'This isn't a Sunday school treat, and these people aren't jokin'. If anythin' happened to Mr. Bellamy — and it's quite likely it may — you and Miss Arbinger'd be responsible. You realise that?'

''ere! 'alf a minute, cock,' interrupted Bellamy angrily. 'It was my idea — '

'I don't care whose idea it was,' said Mr. Budd. 'It was a darned silly one, anyway. You had information at your disposal which might have helped the ends of justice, and you kept it to yourselves. That's an indictable offence. How do you know that this letter which Miss Arbinger produced wasn't a fake?'

'What do you mean?' said Peter.

'I mean,' said Mr. Budd, 'that so far as we know she may be connected with these Silver Horseshoe people. The letter may have merely been for use if anything went wrong.'

'I've never heard such a lot of claptrap!' declared the reporter, flushing. 'Are you suggesting that Miss Arbinger would have connived in the killing of her own father?'

'I've heard of stranger things,' answered Mr. Budd. 'I've met cases of mothers conspiring to kill their own children.'

'If you think Miss Arbinger's got anything to do with the Silver Horseshoe, you're a fool!' snarled Peter.

'I'm not sayin' she has,' retorted the stout man. 'I'm only sayin' you've no proof she hasn't. And don't forget she got five thousand pounds, and nobody knows where it came from.'

'And you're insinuating,' Peter said, glaring at him wrathfully, 'that this money came from the Silver Horseshoe, and that she knows where it came from?'

'I'm suggestin' she might,' drawled Mr. Budd.

'Then you're not only a fool, but a damned fool!' snapped Peter.

'Listen, Mr. Ashton.' The superintendent was angry and his voice was harsh. 'I'm investigatin' a case of murder and blackmail, and I'm not such a fool as to be taken in by a pretty face. Let me finish.' He waved a podgy hand impatiently as Peter opened his mouth to interrupt. 'Miss Arbinger may be all that you think she is. On the other hand she may not. And I say that if she's connected with these Horseshoe people you're the fool, and not I, for helping to keep back information which might be useful to the police.'

Peter took an angry step forward, his hands clenched, but old Bellamy grabbed him by the shoulders and jerked him back. "ere, steady, boy,' he warned. 'There's no need for a rough house.'

'I'm not going to stand by and hear a girl slandered!' said Peter between his teeth. 'Let me go, Jacob.'

But the bookmaker only tightened his grip. 'Budd's right from his point of view, though I think it's a wrong one.'

'It's only natural that you should be annoyed, Mr. Ashton,' said the superintendent, relapsing into his habitual sleepy drawl. 'But I'm talkin' plainly because I'm naturally annoyed, too.'

'Because you're annoyed? There's no

need to make ridiculous accusations!' snapped Peter.

'I haven't made any accusations yet,' said Mr. Budd. 'I've only been pointin' out possibilities. I'm not even sayin' that I believe in them meself.'

'Well, why all that rigmarole?' demanded the reporter.

'Just to show you,' said the stout man, 'how stupid you've been.'

'Well,' said old Jacob, 'suppose we admit we've been stupid. What then?'

'Then,' said Mr. Budd, 'I suggest you bring me another can of this good beer of yours and we'll have a little heart-to-heart talk.'

The suggestion was adopted, and for the greater part of three hours they discussed the situation from every angle. When the stout man finally took his leave Peter accompanied him, and with them went Tony Sellini, an unwilling cog in the machinery which Mr. Budd was laboriously constructing for the ultimate destruction of the Silver Horseshoe.

★ ★ ★

The first day's racing of the season at Gatwick was marked by unusually fine weather, and in consequence the Surrey course was crowded. The going would be better than it had been for many years. The spring rain, alternating with brilliant bursts of sunshine, had favoured the growth of thick young grass, and the course was in almost perfect condition.

Gatwick possesses one of the best straight miles in the country, though it is not a favourite with some horses on account of its undoubted severity. All races up to a mile are run on this 'straight', and as a result no particular advantage is created by position at the gate.

Lord Sevenways reached the course a few minutes before the first race, and after escorting his wife to the stand made his way to the stables to seek his trainer. He had entered Golden Gleam, a promising three-year-old, for the Alexandra Handicap; and although he had very little hope of winning the race, it would give the horse an outing and test its capabilities for more important events later in the season.

As he made his way through the chattering throng in the Paddock, his eyes were downcast and his face looked pale and haggard. He had been a different man since that night when he had stumbled back to his bedroom in Broad Acres, sick at heart and almost disbelieving the evidence of his own eyesight. Wakeful and restless, he had grappled with his problem until, as the grey of dawn came stealing through the window, he had come to his decision. He would say nothing. He would allow his wife to think that he was unaware of that midnight meeting which he had witnessed. There might be others. He would be watchful and vigilant in the future until he had complete proof.

Lady Sevenways noticed his changed appearance and was concerned, but he answered her anxious inquiries with the excuse that he had slept badly. Although she accepted this explanation she was obviously worried, and her worry changed to puzzlement as she noticed the subtle change in his manner. He became stiff and formal, and although his habitual courtesies still remained it seemed to Sybilla as though a barrier, invisible but tangible, had sprung up between them.

Again and again she tried to discover the cause, never guessing for an instant what really lay at the root of the trouble, for she had no suspicion that her husband was aware of her meeting with the man who had come stealthily by appointment to the moonlit grounds of the old house — who had come before and would come again, and in order to meet whom she had told lie after lie.

'Good day, m'lord.' Lord Sevenways looked up, startled out of his unpleasant thoughts, and saw his trainer standing by the entrance to the saddling enclosure.

'Good day, Morgan,' said Sevenways. 'How's Golden Gleam?'

Joe Morgan beamed. 'First-class condition, m'lord,' he answered. 'If it wasn't for Dawn Light I'd say we had a chance.'

'The journey didn't make him nervous?'

'No, he's as cool as a cucumber,

m'lord,' he answered, 'I reckon he'll be in the first three.'

'I shan't particularly mind if he's not,' said Sevenways. 'Tell Rook to give him an easy race.'

The horses were going down to the gate for the first race when he rejoined his wife.

'What does Morgan say? Does he think Golden Gleam has a chance?' she asked, and he nodded. 'Wouldn't it be lovely if we won? 'Her eyes sparkled. 'Have you backed him, Nicky?'

'Only a pony,' he answered dully, scanning the crowd through his glasses. 'I don't think he'll win.'

'But he might,' she said excitedly.

'Well, I took a 100 to 6,' he replied, 'so I shan't do so badly.'

'They're off!' The familiar cry came thundering up as the bell rang and a bunched mass of horse-flesh and silken jackets came hurtling towards the post. The race was over in a flash, for it was only a five-furlong event.

'Who won?' demanded Sergeant Leek, stretching his long neck over the heads of the people in front of him, in an endeavour to catch a glimpse of the number board.

'Whoever it is, you haven't,' grunted Mr. Budd unsympathetically. 'Your horse was last.'

The sergeant's jaw dropped. 'Are you sure?' he asked anxiously. 'I can't follow these 'ere colours, they go so quick.'

'There go the numbers,' said the superintendent, and consulted his card. 'Scotch Mist, one. Moon Love, two. Marica, three. Come on.'

'Where are you going?' asked the sergeant mournfully as he realised that his money had gone to swell the coffers of Mr. Bellamy.

'I'm going to draw my winnings,' answered Mr. Budd complacently. 'I had ten bob each way on Scotch Mist.'

'You might have told me,' said the aggrieved sergeant.

'You wasn't there!' retorted Mr. Budd. 'You was too busy gettin' inside information. Where did you get hold of the idea that Spider Web had a chance?'

'I paid a shillin' for it,' said Leek

gloomily, and his superior gave him a withering look.

'You don't mean to tell me,' he demanded, 'that you've been wastin' money on tipsters?'

'That feller was a foreign prince!' exclaimed Leek. ''e said it was a certainty.'

'It was — for him,' answered Mr. Budd. 'He makes a bob, anyway.'

He halted beside Jacob Bellamy's stand and produced his ticket. As his winnings were handed to him he saw Peter Ashton, accompanied by Marjorie Arbinger.

'Hello!' said the reporter. 'You seem to have been lucky.'

'I've won twenty-five bob,' answered the stout man. 'Not so bad for a beginnin'. Good afternoon, miss.'

The girl acknowledged his greeting coldly. She had not forgotten her father's violent death and still, quite unjustly, attributed it to the laxity of the police. As she turned away to seek Jacob Bellamy, Peter took Mr. Budd to one side. 'Well,' he said in a low voice, 'seen any suspicious characters about?'

'You can't go to any racecourse in the

world without seein' suspicious characters. But if you mean have I seen anyone that I think is likely to be mixed up in the Silver Horseshoe business, no. Maybe there are some in the Silver Ring, but there aren't any in Tattersalls.'

'Well, I hope there won't be,' answered Peter. 'I'd hate anything to happen to old Jacob.'

'Nothing'll happen to Mr. Bellamy. You can take my word for that!' declared Mr. Budd emphatically.

'I've spotted two suspicious-looking fellows,' Peter said seriously. 'They've been hanging about round Bellamy's stand ever since he arrived.' He pointed to two men, immaculately dressed, who were chatting in low tones nearby.

Mr. Budd surveyed them sleepily. 'Sergeant Marshall and Sergeant Burns.'

'Your men?' Peter was surprised.

'Yes. There's two more over there. I'm not takin' any chances, Mr. Ashton, so you needn't worry.'

Peter's relief was evident by his expression. 'Well, I don't see very well how anything can happen now.'

'But I'm hopin' they'll try,' Mr. Budd said. 'I should hate to have gone to all this trouble for nothing. Miss Arbinger didn't look as though she was very pleased to see me.'

'Well, she's naturally a little bit sore,' said Peter.

'Nothing could have saved her father!' declared Mr. Budd. 'Nothin' short of a regiment of soldiers guardin' him from the moment he received that letter. All the same, I understand her feelings . . . Where's that sergeant of mine got to?' He looked round, but the lean form of Leek had disappeared. 'Gettin' more tips from foreign princes, I suppose,' he murmured sarcastically.

'There he is,' said Peter Ashton suddenly, and pointed.

Following the direction of his arm, Mr. Budd saw the lean form of the sergeant over by the stands, talking earnestly to a short, stoutish man who was immaculately dressed in grey.

At that moment the grey man turned so that both he and Peter were able to see his face. It was Mr. Piggott.

9

The Ultimatum

The American saw that he had been recognised, and waved a greeting.

'That feller certainly gets about,' muttered Mr. Budd. He moved over towards the jovial-faced little man, and after a word to Marjorie Arbinger, Peter followed him.

'How d'you do, Superintendent?' greeted Mr. Piggott with a beaming smile. 'Now you're the last man I should have thought would have played the races.'

'I'm not playin' anything,' replied Mr. Budd wearily. 'I'm here on business.'

'Is that so?' Mr. Piggott raised his eyebrows and glanced at Peter. 'Are you here on business, too, Mr. Ashton?'

'In a way,' answered the reporter vaguely.

'Are you here on business?' asked Mr. Budd bluntly, eyeing the stout little man suspiciously.

'Now what business should I have on a racecourse?' inquired Mr. Piggott. 'I'm here for the love of the sport, sir. Purely for the love of the sport.'

Sergeant Leek, who had appeared rather dismayed when he discovered that Mr. Budd and the American knew each other, broke into the conversation. 'He says Inquisitive Lass is a cert for the next race,' he remarked.

'Barring accidents it'll pass the post first,' declared Mr. Piggott confidently. 'I'm a pretty good judge of horse-flesh.'

'I didn't know you two was acquainted,' murmured Mr. Budd.

'I recognised Sergeant Leek and spoke to him,' answered the American. 'I'm naturally of a sociable disposition.'

'So I've noticed. You seem to make friends wherever you go, sir. Partial to detectives, too.'

'I think your police are wonderful!' said Mr. Piggott, and he was openly smiling.

'The bookmakers don't seem to fancy that horse much,' put in Leek, who had been gazing anxiously round. 'It's a hundred to six.'

'Don't let that worry you,' said the American. 'I guess Inquisitive Lass'll walk it.'

'Know a lot about horses?' said Mr. Budd sleepily.

'Just a little,' answered Mr. Piggott.

'I'll bet you do. Particularly horse-shoes.'

'It depends what they're made of.' The smiling face was suddenly grave. 'I'm not particularly interested in iron ones.'

'No, I guessed that,' said Mr. Budd. 'Do you expect to see any of the other sort around here?

'You never know,' said Mr. Piggott. 'Well, I guess I'll be going. I want to back that horse.' He moved away with a cheery nod, and the big man stood gazing after him until he was lost to sight in the crowd.

'That feller's u — whatever the word is,' he remarked.

'Ubiquitous?' suggested Peter.

'That's it, Mr, Ashton.' The superintendent nodded. 'What a thing it is to be a writer.'

'Do you know him?' asked Leek, who

had listened to the conversation with a puzzled expression.

'Yes, I know him,' said Mr. Budd, 'and I'd like to know a lot more. It's a funny thing the way that feller turns up whenever there's likely to be anythin' doin'. He was at the Green Parrot when you was expectin' the feller who set Sellini and his boys on to Mr. Bellamy. And now he's here, just when we're waitin' for somethin' else to happen. Queer! I think it'd be worth findin' out a lot more about Mr. Samuel K. Piggott.'

'He knew me all right,' said the sergeant. 'Addressed me by me name.'

'Did you expect him to address you by somebody else's name?'

'No,' said Leek. 'But I don't recollect ever seein' him before.'

'Well, I expect you'll see him again,' murmured the stout man, 'and maybe it won't be under such pleasant circumstances, either.'

His prophecy came true sooner than any of them expected

'I think I'll have a bit on this horse he was talkin' about,' said Leek. 'I've got to

170

get me money back somehow.'

'Well, don't put it on with Jacob,' said Peter. 'I've got an idea the horse might win, and you don't want to soak him.'

The sergeant peered anxiously round the ring of bookmakers.

'They're all straight,' the reporter assured him.

'Aren't you backin' anythin'?' inquired Leek, and Mr. Budd shook his head.

'I'm not backin' anythin' more today,' he remarked. 'I've won twenty-five bob, and when I win money I keep it.'

Leek went off disconsolately to place his bet, and Mr. Budd accompanied Peter back to where they had left Marjorie Arbinger. The girl was standing by the side of Jacob Bellamy's stand, watching the crowd interestedly. The bookmaker was apparently too busy to more than grunt a word to her now and again, and she welcomed Peter's reappearance with obvious pleasure.

'You have been a long time,' she said. 'Who was that you were speaking to?'

'A queer fellow called Piggott,' said Peter, and she frowned.

171

'D'you mean the man who spoke to you at the club?' she asked, and he nodded. 'What's he doing here?'

'That's what I'd like to know, miss,' remarked Mr. Budd. He moved nearer to the bookmaker.

'Orange Blossom an even pound.' The old man took the money and his clerk made a note of the bet. 'The ticket's thirty-six, sir.' He handed over the slip of pasteboard and the man who had invested his money on Orange Blossom turned away. 'First Again, fifteen to two. Thirty pounds to four. The ticket's thirty-seven.' The clerk scribbled the number of the ticket and the amount in the column headed 'First Again,' and as the bookmaker turned Mr. Budd whispered something. The other shook his head, and the big man rejoined Peter and the girl.

'Nothing's happened yet,' he murmured below his breath. 'Where's that sergeant of mine?' They looked round, but there was no sign of the lugubrious Leek. 'If he'd attend more to his business and less tryin' to make easy money he'd be better off,' grunted Mr. Budd.

'The horses have just gone down to the gate,' said Peter. 'I think I'll have a modest pound on Inquisitive Lass. I think that fellow knew something.'

'I think he knows a lot,' said Mr. Budd. 'And I'm not referring to horses.'

'Who are you speaking about?' asked the girl, and when Peter told her: 'Put me a pound on, too, will you?' She opened her bag and extracted a note, which she passed to him.

'Look after her, Budd, will you? I'll join you in a minute,' he said, and elbowed his way through the crowd. With the girl at his side the stout detective began to walk slowly towards the stands.

'Do you think anything will happen with Bellamy?' she asked after a long silence.

'I'm hopin' so. But Mr. Bellamy won't get hurt. I can promise you that.'

She was not altogether impressed by his assurance, for she had little faith in Mr. Budd's capabilities.

Peter rejoined them as they took their places on the stand, and a minute later the second race began. It was a selling plate for three-year-olds, run over a mile. For a few seconds after the start the nine horses engaged were bunched together, the jockeys' colours indistinguishable, and then two drew away from the ruck and an excited roar went up from the crowd. Peter glanced quickly at his card.

'The green and orange jacket is Inquisitive Lass,' he said. 'And the pink and white hoops is the favourite, Orange Blossom.'

The girl, her lips parted and her eyes sparkling, craned her neck.

'It's a close race,' breathed Peter. 'I think the favourite's going to do it. Yes. Orange Blossom!'

The cry was taken up by the crowd as the pink and white came level with the orange and green and drew ahead. Mr. Budd heard an exclamation near him and saw the lugubrious face of Sergeant Leek. The distance between the two horses increased, and then a streak of brown and scarlet detached itself from the bunch behind.

'First Again! Come on, First Again!'

The comparatively few backers of First Again screamed their excitement, but their shouts were drowned by the thunderous babble that urged the favourite on.

'Orange Blossom's won it!'

But he hadn't. With a burst of surprising speed Inquisitive Lass, her jockey lying almost flat on her out-craned neck, came creeping up alongside. Their colours blended as the two horses flashed past the post.

'Inquisitive Lass! Inquisitive Lass wins!'

The cry was meagre, for the horse had carried very little money.

'Did it win?' Leek put the question eagerly to Peter.

'It looked like a dead heat to me. We shall have to wait till the numbers go up.'

After a short interval they did so.

'Yes, you're all right,' he said. 'And so are we, Marjorie. Inquisitive Lass one. Orange Blossom two. First Again three!'

In the excitement he had called the girl by her Christian name without noticing, but she noticed it, although she made no comment. Leek's melancholy face was less lugubrious than usual.

'I 'ad a quid on it!' he said with satisfaction. 'I'd better go and draw me money before that feller 'ops it.'

'You needn't be afraid of that,' said Peter. But the sergeant was already forcing his way through the crowd. 'I'll go and draw ours,' said the reporter. 'You stay here with Budd.'

'We'll meet you at Mr. Bellamy's stand,' said the stout man, and with a nod Peter made his way down to the ring.

'You don't look very excited,' said the girl, eyeing her sleepy-eyed companion. She was flushed and her eyes were sparkling.

'No, miss, I can't say as I am,' he replied.

'I love it,' she said. 'I think there's nothing more wonderful.'

They crossed the enclosure and came in sight of the huge figure of the bookmaker, busily paying out to the lucky people who had backed Inquisitive Lass. Peter came up to them and handed the girl her winnings.

'It was a wonderful race,' she said, as she put the money away in her bag. 'I — ' She broke off as Mr. Budd uttered a low exclamation.

'Look!' muttered the big man. 'That's the feller we're waitin' for, I think.'

The little knot of people in front of Bellamy's stand had thinned, and approaching it was a smart-looking man in chauffeur's uniform, carrying in one hand a white envelope.

Mr. Budd edged closer and made an almost imperceptible signal to the two loungers who had never moved very far away. They sauntered over until they were within a few yards of the chauffeur.

'Are you Mr. Jacob Bellamy, sir?' The man looked up at the huge figure of the bookmaker and put the question respectfully.

'That's me,' was the reply.

'A gentleman gave me this note,' said the man, holding out the envelope. 'He said there would be a reply.'

The bookmaker took it, ripped open the envelope, and withdrew a card. He gave one glance at it and snapped his fingers. Mr. Budd jerked his head and the two men came up on either side of the startled chauffeur.

'Come along, we want you!' said one of them sternly, and took the man by the arm. 'We're police officers.'

'What's the idea?' demanded the chauffeur indignantly. 'I haven't done anything.' The chauffeur's face was pale and he looked frightened. 'A gentleman asked me to bring a note to Mr. Bellamy and wait for a reply. There ain't nothing wrong in that, is there?'

'You'll see what's wrong in it,' grunted the other detective. 'Keep quiet now and there'll be no trouble.'

Peter and the girl, watching interestedly, saw Mr. Budd take a card from the bookmaker's hand and read it, and consumed with curiosity Peter crossed to his side.

'Is it from the Horseshoe?' he asked. The big man nodded, and without a word held the card out to him.

It was a plain square of thin pasteboard. Typed neatly on one side was the following:

*'Give the thousand pounds to the
bearer of this and there will be no
more trouble. Fail to do so and we
shall carry out our threat.'*

The familiar impression of the horseshoe took the place of a signature.

'Now,' said Mr. Budd, as he took back
the card and placed it carefully in his
pocketbook, 'we'll see what this feller has
to say.'

*   *   *

The chauffeur had a lot to say. In his
fright he became extremely voluble. A
gentleman had come over to him in
the car park and asked him if he would
mind taking a note to Mr. Jacob Bellamy,
the bookmaker, whose stand was in
Tattersalls. He had demurred, but the
gentleman, who had been very pleasant-
spoken, had offered him a fiver; and since
fivers were not too easily come by he had
eventually agreed. The gentleman had
told him to wait for an answer, and that
was all he knew.

'Are you aware what this note contains?' said Mr. Budd sternly.

'I don't know nothing more than I've told you,' said the man. 'I was to take the reply back to the gentleman, who said he'd wait for me in the car park.

'Who's your regular employer?' asked the superintendent.

'Lord Sevenways,' answered the man. 'He's here somewhere.' He looked round. He nodded to where Sevenways was chatting to a little group of men.

'Just a minute.' Mr. Budd moved ponderously across. 'Excuse me, m'lord,' he said, and Sevenways turned in surprise. 'There's a feller here who says he's your chauffeur. Would you mind comin' and identifyin' him?'

'My chauffeur? What the deuce is he doing here?'

Mr. Budd drew him to one side and in a low voice rapidly explained.

'Good Heavens!' gasped Sevenways. 'Certainly I'll come. Excuse me, my dear.' He turned to his wife, who was watching curiously. 'I'll be back in a second.'

He followed Mr. Budd back to where

the chauffeur stood in the care of the detectives. He glanced at the man and nodded.

'Yes, this is my chauffeur,' he said. 'He can't know anything about this business, Superintendent.'

'I'm beginning to think you're right, m'lord,' said Mr. Budd wearily. 'All right, let him go. 'Now,' went on the superintendent, 'I'm rather anxious to meet this man who gave you that note. Do you mind taking a reply back? And we'll foller you.'

'OK,' said the chauffeur.

The fat man stepped over to the bookmaker's stand and returned with a small parcel. 'Here you are,' he said. 'Give him that. I'm sorry to have troubled you, m'lord,' he added, turning to Sevenways.

'That's all right,' said Sevenways. 'Only too glad to have been of assistance . . . Go on, Simpson. Do anything the superintendent tells you.'

The chauffeur touched his hat and turned away. Mr. Budd and the two detectives followed at a respectful distance. The man passed out of the enclosure, skirted the paddock, and entered the car park. Pausing beside a big Bentley, he looked about him, but except for a scattered collection of his own fraternity the place was deserted.

For a quarter of an hour they waited, but nobody put in an appearance, and Mr. Budd gave a sigh. 'I'm afraid we've lost him,' he said, shaking his head sadly. 'He must have had somebody watching, saw what happened to his messenger, and cleared off.' He beckoned to the chauffeur. 'Can you give me a description of this man?' he said.

The chauffeur did his best, but it was not very helpful. He had been of medium height, very well dressed, and aged about thirty-five. His complexion was rather fresh and he had a little fair moustache. 'I'd recognise him again if I saw him,' ended the man confidently.

'You won't see him,' murmured Mr. Budd. 'Nothing is more certain than that.' He came back to where he had left Peter and the girl, a disappointed man.

'Well, what do we do now?' asked the reporter when he was told of the failure.

182

'We watch Bellamy,' said Mr. Budd seriously. 'These people's orders have been disobeyed, and they know it. They've got to do something to keep up their reputation.'

'You mean that Mr. Bellamy is in danger?' Marjorie asked fearfully.

'I've told you before, and I repeat it,' said Mr. Budd, choosing his words carefully, 'that nothing'll happen to Mr. Bellamy.'

'But you said — ' began the girl, but Mr. Budd had turned away and was talking rapidly to his two henchmen.

'What does he mean?' said Marjorie, appealing to Peter.

'I don't know. But you can be certain he's got something at the back of his mind.'

'He looks so — so sleepy,' she said. 'And — and stupid.'

'He may look it, but he's neither,' answered the reporter. 'He's one of the cleverest men at the Yard.'

Mr. Budd came leisurely back. 'Have you seen that sergeant of mine?' he asked irritably.

'Not since he went to collect his money,' Peter answered.

'I've never known anyone so clever at making himself scarce when there's work to be done,' Mr. Budd grumbled.

Lord Sevenways strolled over at that moment. 'Did you find the man?'

'No, m'lord,' said the superintendent wearily.

His lordship frowned. 'Why should these people pick on Simpson?'

'I don't think they picked on your chauffeur particularly,' said Mr. Budd. 'It was just an accident they chose him. They wanted somebody who could hold the baby if anything went wrong. They had somebody watchin' him all the time. If everythin' had gone right the feller who sent him would have been waitin'. But he was tipped off and made himself scarce.'

'Well, I hope you're more successful another time,' said Sevenways. 'Something ought to be done to stop these people.'

His wife called him, and with a hurried 'Coming, my dear', he went back to his party.

'Anybody know anythin' about that feller?' said Mr. Budd, following the thin figure with sleepy eyes.

'Who, Sevenways? He's got a place near my cottage,' answered Peter. 'His wife used to be one of the Ziegfeld Follies. He married her while he was over in America.'

'Got plenty of money, I suppose?' said the stout man.

'No,' answered the reporter. 'Sevenways has scarcely got two pennies to rub together. His father gambled away two fortunes. When he died there was very little left.'

'My father knew him,' said Marjorie. 'He once told me he was the nicest man he'd ever met.'

Mr. Budd was interested. 'And this feller lives near you, Mr. Ashton?'

'Yes,' said Peter. 'At Broad Acres. The border of the estate touches my garden.'

'His wife is certainly very lovely,' said Marjorie, looking towards the slim figure of Lady Sevenways.

'They've got a horse running in the next race,' said Peter. 'Golden Gleam. But

185

the bookmakers are laying twenty to one against it.'

'If Leek gets to hear of that he'll put his shirt on,' said Mr. Budd.

At that moment the lean sergeant put in an appearance.

'Where have you been?' demanded his superior.

'I've been talkin' to a feller over there,' explained Leek. 'He says the winner of the next race is Mornin' Dew.'

'Well, it can be Evenin' Rain for all I care,' growled Mr. Budd. 'You can cut out racin' for the rest of the day, and attend to your legitimate business. Have you seen anythin' of that man Piggott?'

The sergeant shook his thin head. 'No. He seems to have disappeared.'

'Maybe he's got a good reason,' said Mr. Budd.

The betting for the Alexandra Handicap had begun. The horses had finished parading and were moving down towards the tapes.

'Aren't you goin' to see this race?' asked Leek.

'No!' said the superintendent. 'I'm

watchin' for somethin' more important — and I may want you, so you'd better stop here.'

'All right,' said Leek resignedly. 'But it seems a pity.'

'Coming to watch the race?' asked Peter, turning to the girl.

'Yes,' she said. 'I'd like a couple of pounds on Blue Bird. I rather fancy it.'

'Seven to four,' said Peter. 'It's second favourite. Skylark is first favourite. Personally I'm going to have a bit on the outsider, Golden Gleam.'

'Put me ten bob on Mornin' Dew, Mr. Ashton,' said Leek, fumbling in his pocket and producing a crumpled note.

'All right,' said Peter. 'But I think you'll lose your money.'

'D'you think so?' Leek said mournfully. 'Well, p'raps I'd better not risk it.' He returned the note to his pocket.

'We'll see you after the race,' Peter said, and taking the girl by the arm made his way through the crowd.

When he had executed his bet he moved up to the stand, reaching it just as the bell went signalling the 'off.' The race was only six furlongs and, to the surprise of everyone, was won by Golden Gleam. The shouting had barely died down and the stand was emptying when a dull explosion shook the ground.

'What the deuce was that?' muttered Peter, and Marjorie's face went white.

'It came from the enclosure,' she muttered. 'Do you think — '

But Peter was elbowing his way through the crush. He heard the screams of women and the cries of somebody in pain. As he drew near to Jacob Bellamy's stand he caught sight of a blue-coated policeman amid the crowd.

'Now then, stand back!' said an authoritative voice.

'What happened?' Marjorie, breathless, was at Peter's elbow.

'I can't see. Cling on to me.'

He forced his way nearer, then his breath left his lips in a gasp as reaching the fringe of the excited throng, he saw.

A cordon had been formed round the spot which had lately been occupied by the bookmaker's stand. But of the stand nothing was left but a heap of splintered wood and blackened, smouldering canvas. The huge figure of the bookmaker lay sprawled amidst the wreckage, and a pall of smoke drifted sluggishly in the still air.

'My God!' Peter caught sight of Mr. Budd and signalled frantically.

The big man, his face stern and set, came over, and at a word the uniformed policeman allowed him and the girl to break the cordon.

'What was it?' whispered Peter, aghast.

'A bomb!' said Mr. Budd grimly.

'And Bellamy — is — is he dead?'

'No, sir,' Mr. Budd answered. 'He ain't dead. He isn't even injured.'

'Then what the deuce is he lying there for?' demanded Peter, turning his eyes towards the still figure that lay motionless amid the ruins of the stand.

'He isn't,' said Mr. Budd. 'That's not Jacob Bellamy, and it never was Jacob Bellamy. That's Sergeant Gayling, and he's as dead as don't matter!'

10

The Men of the Night

Several people had been injured by flying particles of metal and a number of women had fainted from shock. The ambulance men were kept busy attending to the wounded, and in the general confusion and excitement which followed the unprecedented occurrence Peter found no opportunity to speak to Mr. Budd again for some time.

Marjorie was horrified, but relieved when she learned that Jacob Bellamy was uninjured. The rugged old bookmaker had found a place in her affections, although she had known him but a short while. Peter got her out of the crowd and escorted her to the luncheon tent, and then went back to find out all he could concerning the outrage.

'It must have been a time bomb,' said Mr. Budd when he eventually succeeded in getting hold of that harassed official. 'Not a very powerful one, luckily, but enough to do what was intended. Somebody succeeded in slipping it under the stand without being seen. Not a very difficult thing to do in this crowd. Luckily there was nobody near the stand when the thing went off.'

'What about the clerk?' asked Peter.

'He wasn't there,' said the detective, shaking his head. 'He'd gone away for a few minutes. I'm sorry about Sergeant Gayling. He was a nice chap. Poor feller.'

'Why didn't you tell me it wasn't Bellamy?' demanded the reporter.

'Because I thought the fewer people who knew about it the better,' said Mr. Budd. 'I had great difficulty in persuading Mr. Bellamy to keep away. In fact I nearly had to lock him up.'

'He was very like old Jacob,' muttered Peter. 'I had no suspicion — '

'He was like enough. Sufficiently so, anyway, to deceive these people. I suppose you're goin' to print an account of this business in that rag of yours?'

'You bet your life I am!' said Peter. 'Old

Sorbet'll dance with joy when he hears.'

The Stewards had arrived, three anxious and horrified men, and Mr. Budd went off to pacify their righteous indignation.

Peter waited until he learned that racing was to be abandoned for the rest of the day, and then he sought out a telephone and poured into Mr. Sorbet's willing ears an account of the tragedy. When he had done this he went back to find the girl, and put a suggestion which had occurred to him.

'When Budd is through here, suppose we go back to my cottage? It's quiet there. It'll only take half an hour. We can talk without being disturbed.'

She agreed, and he hurried away to find the superintendent.

'I ought to go back to the Yard,' Mr. Budd demurred.

'Well, you can later,' urged Peter. 'Come along. I think we ought to have a conference over this.'

The big man agreed eventually. 'I tell you what you might do, Mr. Ashton,' he said. 'Telephone Bellamy and ask him to come down to your place. You'll find him at the Yard. I arranged with him to stop there all day.'

'All right, I'll do that,' said Peter. 'How long will you be before you're through?'

'I'll be some time,' Mr. Budd murmured. 'It's three-thirty now . . . I shan't be ready before half-past four.'

'That'll do,' said Peter. 'Meet me in the refreshment tent.' He went back to the telephone, got on to the Yard, and a few seconds later was talking to old Jacob Bellamy.

'It's disgraceful, cock!' said the old man, when Peter finished his account. 'Somethin's got to be done to put these people where they can't do any more harm.'

'Budd wants you to come down to my cottage,' said Peter. 'We're going to have a conference. If you leave now you'll get there about the same time as we shall.' He gave explicit directions.

'All right, boy, I'll find it,' said the old man. 'Has that poor feller who took my place got any family, or anyone dependent on him?'

'I don't know,' said Peter.

'Well, find out, will yer?' said old Bellamy. 'Because if so I'm goin' to look after 'em. It's the only thing I can do. So long, cock. See you later.'

Peter returned to the refreshment room. Marjorie was looking white and shaken and he insisted that she should have a brandy and soda and a sandwich. He was beginning to feel the reaction himself.

'It was a ghastly thing!' said the girl. 'Those people can't be human.'

Mr. Budd and the lugubrious Leek put in an appearance just after half-past four, and the four of them made their way to Peter's car. It was a tight squeeze, but they managed it, and set off for Peter's little weekend retreat.

It was a quarter past five when they reached the cottage, and they found old Jacob Bellamy waiting in the little garden. Peter unlocked the door, shepherded them into the tiny sitting room, and set about making tea. Marjorie insisted on helping him, and when they were all supplied with tea and biscuits Peter opened the subject which was uppermost in all their minds.

'Well,' he said, 'what's the next move?'

'I don't know, Mr. Ashton,' said the superintendent. 'We don't know who these people are or who's at the back of them.'

'Well,' growled Jacob, 'we've got to find out. You can't tell me that a group of people can get away with murder and not be punished for it.'

'I'm not,' said the stout man. 'But it may take some time, Mr. Bellamy.'

To the surprise of everyone it was Sergeant Leek who supplied the most sensible contribution to the discussion.

'It seems to me,' he said mournfully, 'that this horseshoe lot have the advantage because they know us and we don't know them.'

'That's obvious,' grunted Mr. Budd.

'What I mean is,' continued the sergeant, 'couldn't we pretend to be doin' somethin' that we ain't while all the while we're doin' somethin' else?'

'You've got it all mixed up,' said Mr. Budd, 'but I think I can see what you're gettin' at. You mean, can't we lead 'em off on a false trail.'

'That's it!' said Leek eagerly. 'You know when you're followin' a man and you think you're doin' it grand, and all the while, without you knowin' it, someone's followin' you? Can't we do somethin' like that?'

'It's an idea,' echoed Peter. 'But how are we going to do it?'

'Sellini,' said Mr. Budd. 'Sellini's the feller.'

'How d'you mean?' asked the reporter.

'Give me a minute or two, Mr. Ashton,' said the big man, closing his eyes, 'an' I'll tell you.'

It was nearer fifteen than the two minutes he had asked for before he opened his eyes and surveyed them through half-closed lids. 'Now,' he said, in his slow, deliberate manner, 'listen to me.'

They listened while he expounded at some length his scheme. When he had finished, Jacob Bellamy drew a long breath.

'That's darned smart!' he said.

'I'm pretty good at these kinds of

things,' Mr. Budd said, smiling immodestly. 'Strategy is one of my strong points. But you've got to promise me, all of you, that you won't go off on any wild-cat schemes of your own. I don't mind you helpin', but you've got to tell me everythin'. Is that a bet?'

There was a certain amount of argument concerning this, particularly from Marjorie, but the promise that he wanted was eventually reluctantly given by all of them.

'Now,' Mr. Budd said, 'let's go over this scheme of mine again and see if anyone can suggest any improvement.'

They became so interested in the discussion that followed that they lost track of time. It was only the growing darkness of the room that alerted them to its passage.

'D'you know it's nearly half past nine, cock?' broke in old Bellamy. 'I ought to be gettin' back.'

'So ought I,' said Marjorie.

'I'll drive you back.' Peter struck a match and lit the oil lamp. 'Will you have a drink before — ' He broke off as Leek uttered an exclamation.

'Who's that in your garden, Mr. Ashton?' he said suddenly. 'There's somethin' movin'. I can just see — '

'Put out the lamp!' The sharp, insistent order came from Mr. Budd, no longer sleepy and lethargic, but remarkably alert.

Even as he spoke there was a sudden rush of footsteps, the crash of breaking glass, and silhouetted outside the shattered window they saw the figures of three men.

Marjorie gave a choking scream.

'Keep still! Don't move, any of you!' snarled a muffled voice, and they saw that the thing which had broken the glass was the ugly muzzle of a sub-machine gun.

*   *   *

The occupants of the little sitting room stood rigid as though suddenly turned to stone. Mr. Budd was breathing heavily, his eyes fixed on the shadowy figures outside the window. Marjorie, one hand gripping Peter's arm convulsively, was staring in the same direction, her face drained of colour. Leek, his jaw dropped and an expression of horrified dismay on his long face, eyed the muzzle of the gun apprehensively.

'I guess you're for it!' said the muffled voice of the spokesman. 'A nice bag, boys! All the birds with one stone. What a bit of luck!'

'Who are you?' demanded Peter Ashton, his voice husky with fear for the girl whose fingers gripped so tightly on his arm.

'That's no concern of yours, Mr. Nosey-reporter!' retorted the man with the gun. 'You've stuck your ugly mug into other people's business for the last time! You're going out, the way Arbinger went out! All five of you!'

'So you was responsible for the killing of Mr. Arbinger, was you?' remarked Mr. Budd, his voice conversational and gentle. 'That's somethin' worth knowin'.'

'A lot of good the knowledge will do you!' snarled the man at the window. 'You've got about five seconds left, Fatty!'

'There's no need to get personal,'

murmured the big man, and not by so much as an eyelash did he betray his concern.

They were unarmed, in a lighted room, covered with a gun that could spray death on pressure of the finger which was crooked round the trigger.

In the light of the lamp he could see that the reason for the muffled sound of the man's voice was due to a black handkerchief which had been bound round his face, leaving only his eyes exposed. His two companions were similarly masked.

'You're part of this Horseshoe racket, I suppose?' he asked, more in a desperate attempt to gain time than because there was any necessity for an answer.

'You've spilled a mouthful!' said the masked man. 'And I reckon it's the last mouthful you're going to spill — unless they allow talking in Hell!' He leaned a little forward, and Peter saw the forefinger crooked round the trigger move.

Almost mechanically he jerked the girl behind him, though he knew the action was futile. No one could escape the hail of bullets that the next second would bring.

'My God!' breathed old Bellamy. 'I'm not goin' to die without makin' a fight for it!'

He sprang forward, and the muzzle of the machine-gun belched flame.

Involuntarily Peter closed his eyes. He felt something splattering about him and waited for the red-hot agony that would tell him he had been hit. But it never came. Instead he heard the throaty voice of Mr. Budd utter a surprised exclamation. The rat-tat-tat-tat of the machine-gun suddenly stopped. There were confused shouts, and a pandemonium of noise, and he opened his eyes to see the superintendent, covered in white plaster, make for the window.

A shot, outside and close at hand, reached his ears.

'Grab that gun and follow me!' snapped the big man as, heedless of the broken glass, he began to scramble through the shattered window.

Completely bewildered, the reporter

201

saw the machine-gun lying amid a litter of plaster, and glancing up discovered it had come from the riddled ceiling. What had happened he was unable to guess, but for some reason or other the man in the mask had done no more harm than to pit the ceiling with bullets. He moved forward to pick up the gun, and found the girl clinging to him.

'Don't go!' she panted breathlessly. 'Don't go!'

'It's all right, kid,' said old Jacob. 'Those blighters have sheered off.'

'What happened?' muttered Peter.

'I dunno, cock — but just as that feller pulled the trigger he jerked his gun upwards, and then they all turned and flew for their lives.'

Another shot came from outside, followed by the voice of Mr. Budd. 'There they are! Over by the hedge!'

'Come on,' said Peter. 'I'm going to be in this.' He snatched up the gun. 'You stop here, Marjorie. You'll be all right. Look after her, Jacob, will you?'

'Can't I join in?' he pleaded.

'Yes — you go with Mr. Ashton. I'll be

all right.' Marjorie had got a grip on her nerves.

Peter flung up the sash, swung his legs over the sill, and disappeared into the darkness, with Bellamy at his heels. A volley of shots rang out, and a huge figure loomed in front of them. Peter swung up his gun.

'Look out with that thing!' said the voice of Mr. Budd. 'I've had enough of it for one evenin'!'

'Which way did they go?' demanded Peter.

'I dunno. I lost 'em,' Mr. Budd muttered.

'There's one!' cried old Jacob, pointing to a blot of shadow creeping along by the hedge.

'Make sure it isn't Leek,' said the superintendent as Peter dashed off towards the moving blot. 'He ain't much good alive, but he'd be less useful dead.'

The whine of a car reached Peter's ears as he drew level with the shadow in the hedge.

'Stop!' he ordered, raising the heavy

gun. 'I want to have a look at you, my friend!'

The man stopped.

'You can have a look at me without threatening me with that thing.'

Peter almost dropped his weapon as he recognised the voice of Mr. Piggott.

'Who is it?' Jacob Bellamy came panting up with Mr. Budd.

'It's that fellow Piggott!' answered Peter grimly.

'So he was in it, was he?' Mr. Budd asked.

'Yes, I was in it, sir,' said the American. 'You ought to be very thankful that I *was* in it, otherwise I rather guess you'd be dead meat by now — all of you!'

'Weren't you one of those men at the window?' demanded the reporter.

'I was *not*,' answered the American. 'But I wasn't very far away. If I hadn't slugged that feller with the gun just as he was going to open fire you'd have been a nasty mess.'

'Come and do a little explaining,' suggested Mr. Budd.

Piggott moved towards them; and

Peter, alert and suspicious, followed his movements with the muzzle of the gun.

'I wish you'd put that thing away,' said the American plaintively. 'But if you're scared of any monkey tricks I don't mind obliging you by holding my arms above my head in the approved manner.' He suited the action to the words, and Peter lowered the heavy gun.

'That's better!' said 'Superstitious Sam'. 'I feel much more comfortable.'

They went back to the house and as Peter saw the girl in the open window he called to her to go round and unlatch the door. She obeyed, and when they reached the sitting room Mr. Budd turned to the captive.

'Now,' he said, 'spill it! Was that you who was doin' the firin'?'

'I guess it was,' said Mr. Piggott. He dropped his hand into the pocket of his coat and produced an automatic. 'It's all right,' he said with a smile as Peter made a gesture with his gun. 'It's empty now. I used the last shot trying to wing one of those fellows.'

'D'you mean you weren't with them?' demanded the reporter.

'Haven't I told you so?' Piggott said plaintively. 'I saw what was happening, and I was just in time to spoil their little game. I think I got that tall fellow in the arm,' he added musingly.

'So that's what made his gun jerk up,' grunted Mr. Budd. 'I never heard the shot.'

'I'm under the impression that it coincided with his first shot.' Mr. Piggott looked up. 'Made a nasty mess of the ceiling, hasn't it? Still, it would have made a nastier mess if those slugs had gone anywhere else.'

'What were you doin' here?' Mr. Budd asked.

'Just taking an evening stroll, sir,' said Mr. Piggott innocently.

'I see,' murmured Mr. Budd. 'And that's all the explanation you're goin' to give, eh?'

'Surely it's sufficient? You've got a naturally suspicious nature, Superintendent.'

'Maybe I have,' replied Mr. Budd. 'It's

a good way from here to Gatwick.'

The American smiled. 'I came by car, sir. It's parked outside the inn in the village.'

'An' you was just strollin' around,' murmured Mr. Budd, 'and turned up in the nick of time. Remarkable!'

'Lucky,' corrected Mr. Piggott. 'If I was a religious man I should call it Providence.'

'There are other things it could be called,' said the stout man.

Piggott started. 'What was that?' he asked curtly, and they heard the sound that had disturbed him, the crunch of a footstep outside.

Alert and watchful, they faced the window. Into the dim rays of the lamp came the figure of a man, his white shirt-front startlingly clear. Peter took a tighter grip on the butt of the gun, and then his fingers relaxed as he recognised Lord Sevenways.

'Is there any trouble?' asked his lordship querulously. 'I was walking in my grounds when I heard the sound of shooting. What's been happening?'

Mr. Budd gave the others a warning glance. 'Nothin' very much, sir,' he answered. 'Mr. Ashton was takin' a few pot-shots at some rabbits.'

'They were pistol shots I heard,' said Sevenways suspiciously. 'You don't shoot rabbits with pistols.'

'He was tryin' to prove to us what a good shot he is.' Mr. Budd had moved to Peter's side so that his bulk concealed the machine-gun.

'Well, I'm glad it was nothing serious,' said Sevenways. 'I was afraid there was some trouble. Good night!' He moved away, and they heard his footsteps receding in the distance.

'Why did you tell him that story about rabbits?' asked Peter, and Mr. Budd shrugged his broad shoulders.

'No need to alarm him unnecessarily,' he said. 'And we don't want to make a song about tonight.'

'I think you're wise, sir,' said Mr. Piggott. 'That gentleman was Lord Sevenways, wasn't it?'

'Yes,' answered Peter, and the American sighed.

'He's got a lot to answer for,' he said sadly.

'Just what do you mean by that?' asked Mr. Budd.

'I mean,' replied Mr. Piggott gravely, 'that if it hadn't been for Lord Sevenways there'd have been no Silver Horseshoe. No, sir! That fellow is responsible for all the trouble! You'd never think so to look at him, would you?'

11

The Sentence

The car sped along the dark country road, its dim headlights scarcely serving to more than accentuate the blackness. It bumped erratically on the uneven surface, and the man who drove swore below his breath.

'Can't you be more careful?' snarled the man who sat in the back. 'My arm's hurting like hell!'

'Blame the feller who made these roads!' grunted the driver.

The third man who sat beside him turned in his seat. 'There's going to be trouble over tonight,' he said. 'The chief'll be sore!'

'Not so sore as my blasted arm!' retorted the wounded man. 'Anyhow, it wasn't our fault. How were we to know they had somebody outside with a gun?'

'Who was it?' grunted the driver.

'How the hell should I know?' was the irritable answer.

'We've lost the typewriter, too,' murmured the third man. 'That's going to get us in bad.'

Silence, broken only by the hissing of the tyres and the drumming of the powerful engine.

'How much further is this place we're making for?' said the man at the back suddenly.

The driver glanced down at a map, which was illumined by a dim light on the dashboard. A small circle of red had been drawn amid the spidery lines.

'About four miles now, I guess.'

'What's it this time?' asked the man beside him.

'Empty house,' said the driver laconically.

They passed through a small village, slowing in order to avoid any possibility of a hold-up, came out into open country again, and returned to their former speed. They flashed by a signpost at four crossroads and swung to the left. The road now was narrower, with grass

211

borders and high hedges.

'There should be an openin' along here,' muttered the driver, peering to his right. He turned into a lane and the car bumped heavily over the rutted surface. At each jolt the man in the back cursed volubly.

'Here we are!' The driver slowed and turned in between two crumbling brick pillars. The dim light revealed a curving drive overgrown with neglected shrubbery and dense weeds.

The driver pulled up in front of the sagging porch and got down. The other two alighted with him and followed him to a blistered door that was almost hidden in the masses of creepers and ivy that smothered it. There was a rusty knocker in the centre of the almost paintless panel, and on this the driver of the car gave a peculiar knock.

At length the door opened an inch. 'Who's that?' asked a voice.

'Mayne!' grunted the driver.

'Come in. Are the others with you?' A chain rattled and the door opened wider.

Mayne crossed the threshold, accompanied by his two companions. The man who had opened the door was invisible in the darkness.

'Is it safe to leave the lights on?' said the man who had complained about his wounded arm.

'No! Who left them on?' snarled the doorkeeper.

'I forgot,' muttered Mayne.

'Well, go and put them out!' ordered the other sharply. 'You fool! We don't want the cops snooping round!'

Mayne muttered something below his breath, and going back to the car extinguished the dim lights. When he returned his two companions had disappeared.

'Go straight ahead,' whispered the doorkeeper as he shut the portal. 'Here, take this.'

'This' was a torch, over the lens of which had been pasted a layer of tissue paper so that it gave a barely perceptible light. It was sufficient, however, for the other to pick his way over the dirty, bare boards towards the closed door facing the one by which he had entered. Opening this, he found himself in a large room lit dimly by a single candle that guttered on the mantelpiece. It was quite bare of furniture and the paper was peeling on the grimy walls. Over the windows the wooden shutters had been secured so that no ray of light could percolate outside.

Leaning against the mantelpiece, and facing four other men who were standing in a little group, was the man who called himself J. Stanmore. He was speaking as Mayne entered.

'Two failures in one day is bad.' His voice was suave. 'You've got to do better than this, Tracey.'

The tall man, rubbing his wounded arm, muttered something.

'There were three of you,' the suave voice continued. 'Sufficient to have dealt with any emergency.'

'We didn't expect there'd be anybody lurking about the garden,' said Tracey. 'And when I lost the gun I thought we'd better make a bolt for it.'

'You had the chance of a lifetime. The two policemen, Bellamy and Ashton,' said the man called Stanmore. 'And you bungled it. Surely it didn't want three of you at the window. You should have left two to cover your retreat.'

'I guess if you'd had a bullet through your shoulder — ' began Tracey, but the other interrupted him.

'Who was this man?'

'We didn't see him. The first I knew he was there was when me arm went bust. I dropped the Tommy gun. He must have been somebody left on watch.'

'It's a nuisance!' The man before him frowned, and although he spoke perfect English there was the faintest possible trace of an American accent, just the tinge of a nasal intonation. 'The Bellamy job was bungled this afternoon, and now this. You're in charge of this section, Tracey. It's your job to carry out instructions.'

'How was anybody to know the fellow wasn't Bellamy?' demanded Tracey, not unreasonably. 'I arranged for the bomb all right, didn't I? And Belter slipped it under the stand without being seen.'

'There's something in what you say.'

Stanmore nodded thoughtfully. 'We've got to get them! That man, Budd and Ashton are likely to be a nuisance. They've got to be wiped out. They and Bellamy!'

'That feller's tough!' growled Tracey, wincing as a stab of pain shot through his wounded shoulder. 'Look what happened to Sellini — '

'Sellini!' The contempt in Stanmore's voice was cutting. 'Scared of his own shadow!' He pulled out a cigarette case, extracted a cigarette and lighted it. 'We'll get Bellamy, and we'll get him good!' he went on confidently. 'I've got a scheme.' He began to speak rapidly, and the little group of unpleasant-looking men gathered round him, listening. When he had finished Tracey nodded.

'I'll hand it to you,' he said admiringly, 'it's a cinch!'

'Yes,' said Stanmore. 'They'll fall for it, all right! The English are overly sentimental and quixotic.'

'And when we've got 'em?'

'They die!' said the other calmly. 'The plan will be worked out in detail and you'll receive your instructions in the usual way. And this time I reckon it won't go wrong.'

★   ★   ★

The bomb outrage at Gatwick created a sensation among the general public. The incident was seized upon with avidity by the newsmongers of Fleet Street, and every morning and evening paper came out with banner headlines and a lurid account of the tragedy. They out-vied each other in sensationalism, but the *Morning Mail* and the *Evening Comet* were easily in the lead. Peter Ashton's eyewitness account was a masterpiece of modern journalism, and Mr. Sorbet experienced a glow of satisfaction such as came to him rarely.

Mr. Budd was not so enthusiastic. A number of the other papers carried acrid comments on the administration of Scotland Yard, and hinted broadly that there must be a certain amount of laxity for such things to be possible. The immediate result was a hastily called conference to which the stout superintendent was summoned.

He went in with some trepidation. Colonel Blair, the assistant commissioner, was presiding at the head of the long table, and three stern-faced chief constables surveyed the big man as he took his place.

'We have called you,' began the assistant commissioner without preliminary, 'to hear an explanation for what occurred yesterday. We have lost one of our best men in Sergeant Gayling, and the perpetrators of the outrage remain at large. It's bad, Superintendent. Very bad indeed!'

'I know, sir.' Mr. Budd, from past experience, was aware that any form of argument was useless. 'Nobody realises that better than I do. I was prepared for almost anything but a bomb.'

'I think you should have been prepared for *all* emergencies,' said a grey-haired chief constable reprovingly. 'What steps are you taking to apprehend these people?'

The big man cleared his throat and

began to speak slowly and carefully. He was listened to with attention, and when he had finished Colonel Blair gave a nod of approval.

'In my opinion, Superintendent,' he said, 'that is a very sound idea. We realise the difficulties of dealing with an organisation of this description. At the same time it is essential that something should be done to reassure the public. This is the second spectacular crime they have committed and succeeded in getting away with. There must not be a third. You understand that?'

'I naturally can't guarantee there won't be, sir,' Mr. Budd said. 'But I'll do my best to prevent it.'

'Well, no man can do more,' said Colonel Blair, who was fair, if something of a martinet.

They went into further details concerning Mr. Budd's plan, and then the conference broke up and the big man went ponderously back to his office.

'How'd you get on?' inquired the melancholy Leek.

'It was better'n what I expected,'

replied his superior, seating himself carefully in his padded chair and producing one of his long, black, acrid-smelling cigars, and lighting it. 'I've got a little job for you,' he went on, trickling a stream of smoke from the corner of his mouth.

Leek showed no enthusiasm. 'What is it?' he muttered.

'I want you to go to Broad Acres and keep an eye on this feller Sevenways. I don't want him to know he's bein' watched, you understand, but just follow him wherever he goes, and make a note o' what he does and who he sees.'

'You surely don't think a lord's got anythin' to do with this Horseshoe business, do you?' Leek inquired, aghast.

'Well, lords ain't very much different to other men,' said his superior. 'And there's somethin' queer.'

'I shouldn't go too much on what that feller Piggott says,' the sergeant remarked. 'If you go stirring up trouble with a lord you'll get it in the neck.'

'You'll get it in the neck, too, if you don't do as you're told,' said Mr. Budd coolly. 'I'm not settin' any store on what that American feller said, although I'm rememberin' it for future use. I'm merely usin' me own intelligence, somethin' you wouldn't understand. But here's a feller who was broke until a few weeks ago and now he's got money from somewhere, and I want to know where that somewhere is.'

'Maybe somebody's died and left it him.'

'Maybe somebody has,' said Mr. Budd significantly. 'I'm thinkin' maybe the death of John Arbinger had a lot to do with it.'

The idea that a man of Lord Sevenways's standing and social position could possibly be mixed up in a blackmail racket was beyond Leek's imagination. 'I think you're makin' a mistake,' he protested feebly.

'Well, if I am,' said Mr. Budd, 'it's my responsibility. All you've got to do is what I tell you. And don't make a mess of it. I'm inquirin' very carefully into the history of this feller Sevenways, and I've got a hunch I shan't be wastin' me time.'

How true that hunch was he was to realise before many days had passed.

'Now you get off,' he said. 'I've arranged with Mr. Ashton for the use of his cottage. You can make that your headquarters, and Sergeant Eaton'll come down later so as to relieve you.'

The unhappy sergeant departed, and when he had gone Mr. Budd became a very busy man indeed. Picking up the house telephone, he put through half a dozen calls to various departments and interviewed a number of men whose duties covered a wide and varied field. To each he gave detailed instructions regarding what he wanted, and when he had finished with the last he drew a sheet of paper towards him and wrote out a long cable. When this had been dispatched he leaned back in his chair with a sigh of relief.

He was apparently sleeping when Peter Ashton was announced. 'Sorry to disturb your nap,' said the reporter.

'I wasn't sleeping,' said Mr. Budd severely, opening one eye. 'I was thinkin'.'

Peter smiled. 'I'm meeting Miss Arbinger for tea at the Metro Palace, and I thought perhaps you'd like to come along.'

'That's very kind of you, Mr. Ashton. How is she after last night's experience?'

'She's getting over the shock,' replied Peter. 'What did you make of that fellow Piggott's remark concerning Sevenways being responsible for the Silver Horseshoe?'

'What did *you* make of it?'

'I didn't take it seriously,' Peter said with a shrug. 'He wouldn't explain what he meant, so I concluded that he was just trying to be funny.'

'No, Mr. Ashton. That feller wasn't exhibitin' his sense of humour. He was serious.'

'But Lord Sevenways couldn't have anything to do with a gang of American crooks!'

'My sergeant's under the same impression,' he said. 'But I've always said from the beginnin' that when we get to the bottom of this Silver Horseshoe business we'll get a surprise.'

'We've had a few already,' said Peter.

'And the biggest surprise of all will be

when we find out what's really behind this racket.'

'That's simple — money!' said the reporter.

'Money's only part of it,' said Mr. Budd, suppressing a yawn. 'There's somethin' else ... and that's what interests me.'

'Well, I don't think you'd be far wrong if you arrested Piggott,' declared Peter. 'I'll admit he saved our lives last night, but he knows way too much for my liking.'

'There's nothing we could arrest him for,' said Mr. Budd, shaking his head. 'And there'd be hell to pay if we made a mistake. He's an American citizen, and his consul 'ud soon be raisin' Cain.'

'Well, I still don't think he's as innocent as he makes out.' Peter glanced at his watch and went on: 'Time we were going if we're to meet Marjorie at four o'clock.'

Mr. Budd sighed wearily and hoisted himself out of his chair.

The lounge of the Metro Palace contained the usual smattering of people, but there was no sign of the girl. They waited until a quarter past four and then Peter began to get impatient. 'What can have happened to her?'

'She's only fifteen minutes late,' Mr. Budd murmured. 'That's nothin' in my experience of women. If she gets here by five she'll think she's early.'

They waited another quarter of an hour, and then Peter's impatience changed to uneasiness. 'I'll ring up and see if she's left,' he said, and went over to a row of public call boxes.

He was back in less than three minutes, his face drawn. 'There's something wrong,' he said huskily. 'You didn't send a man for her at half past three, did you?'

Mr. Budd sat up, his sleepy eyes wide open. 'No!' he snapped. 'Why?'

'They tell me that a man called for her at half past three,' said Peter. 'He said he was from Scotland Yard, and Marjorie left with him in a car. Where are you going?' he demanded, for the big man was moving with surprising rapidity towards the exit.

'I'm goin' to Putney,' said Mr. Budd grimly. 'I don't like the sound of it, Mr. Ashton. I don't like the sound of it at all!'

225

12

What Happened to Marjorie

Marjorie Arbinger had no misgivings when the message was brought to her that a detective from Scotland Yard had called to take her to headquarters as Superintendent Budd wanted to ask her some questions.

'If Mr. Ashton rings up tell him where I've gone,' she instructed her maid, and went upstairs to put on her things. A thick-set man was waiting in the hall.

'I'm sorry to trouble you, Miss Arbinger,' he said, 'but the matter is rather urgent, and the superintendent thought you wouldn't mind. I've got a car waiting outside.'

'I don't mind at all,' said the girl. 'Let's go.'

The maid opened the door and he led the way down the short flight of steps to the car that was waiting in the drive.

Opening the door, he waited for her to get in, and then with a word to the man at the wheel took his place beside her. She heard the engine spring to a swifter hum and saw through the side window her maid closing the front door of the house. Then something was jabbed sharply into her arm, she felt everything spin around her, and lost consciousness.

It was a long time before she opened her eyes. A racking pain was crawling to life in her nerves and her head throbbed monotonously. Her heart was beating a thunderous tattoo, which was repeated in her temples, and her skin was hot and clammy. She felt weak and ill.

She discovered presently that she was lying on something soft, but when she tried to get up the effort was beyond her; her muscles refused to obey the command of her brain. It was like a nightmare she had experienced, when everything seemed unreal. Her limbs felt leaden and ached intolerably. There was a light somewhere that hurt her eyes and made her feel sick. She closed them and allowed herself to relax, and slipped back into a state of semiconsciousness. The drug which had been administered to her was still active in her veins.

When she woke again she woke to full consciousness; and like a flood, her memory came quickly and sharply. With a violent effort of will she sat up, clenched her teeth as the movement made her head swim dizzily, and let her eyes wander vaguely about her.

She was lying on a heap of cushions, on some sort of fixed couch at one side of a large, oblong, low-ceilinged room. There was a table and a wooden chair, but the rest of the furniture seemed to be composed of cupboards. Above her head a round light was fixed in the ceiling, and she saw that the windows of this strange apartment were also circular.

The gentle noise of lapping water came to her ears, and then she understood.

She was on board a boat of some description!

She rose to a sitting position and waited for a moment, resting her head in her hands. The dizziness passed away. She looked at her watch. Ten minutes past six, and she had left her house at half past three. Where was she, and what had happened? Of course — the detective! The man who had come to take her to Scotland Yard! Some drug must have been administered to her in the car. But why had she been brought on board this boat?

As she grew stronger, the desire for knowledge increased in equal ratio. She began to explore the place. There was a door at one end of the cabin, or whatever it was, and this she tried, but it was securely fastened. Neither could she see anything through the port-hole-like windows. They were shuttered on the outside. She went back to the bunk and sat down again.

Her throat felt dry and rough. She remembered her appointment with Peter Ashton. Would he ring and find out from her maid what had happened? She felt sure he would, and he would notify the police at once.

She had no doubt concerning the reason for her abduction. A moment's thought convinced her that she had fallen into the hands of the Silver Horseshoe. She was a prisoner at the mercy of the people who had killed her father.

Then she heard the sound of feet outside the door, and shrank away, her eyes fixed on the entrance. A key rattled, and the narrow door opened. The tall man who came in was a stranger to her.

'You needn't be afraid — yet,' he said in a low voice, as he closed the door behind him.

'Why have you brought me here?' she asked.

'I have brought you here,' he replied, 'in order to effect a little bargaining. There are friends of yours who are becoming a nuisance. I propose to barter your safety in exchange for their inactiveness. In other words, I propose to keep you here until they give up their campaign against the Silver Horseshoe.'

'So *you* are the Silver Horseshoe!' she whispered.

'No . . . but I am *of* the Silver Horseshoe.'

'You were responsible for the murder of my father!' she cried.

'I was aware of it but not responsible,' he answered curtly.

'Who are the friends you refer to?' she asked, although she knew very well.

'The reporter, Peter Ashton,' he replied. 'Superintendent Budd and Jacob Bellamy.'

'But how can I stop them?' she demanded. 'What good will keeping me here do you?'

'You will write a letter to your friend the reporter and tell him that you are safe and that you will remain unharmed so long as he and the others agree to discontinue their activities against us.'

'And if they refuse?' she challenged.

'If they refuse you can tell them that you will lose one of your fingers.'

Marjorie stared at him in horror. 'You wouldn't do it! You couldn't do it!' she whispered.

He shrugged. 'Possibly it won't be necessary,' he answered. 'I hope for your sake it won't. But if it is, I assure you that my threat will be carried out.'

He crossed to a cupboard, opened it, and took out a bottle of ink, a pad of paper, and a packet of envelopes. Coming back, he set them down on the table and pulled out the chair.

'I think,' he said, 'you had better do as I ask.'

★ ★ ★

A taxi took Mr. Budd and Peter to Putney, and throughout the journey the big man sat silent and stern, with no sign of his usual sleepiness. When they reached the house on Putney Hill, Peter was out of the cab almost before it had stopped and pulling violently at the bell.

An angry servant answered his summons. 'What d'you mean — ' she began, and then, when she saw who it was: 'Oh, it's you, sir. I thought it was — '

'Somebody called for Miss Arbinger. Who was it?' demanded the reporter, cutting short the girl's explanation.

'A detective from Scotland Yard, sir.' The maid stared at him in mingled astonishment and annoyance. 'She went away with him in a car.'

'What was this man like?' asked Mr.

Budd, breathing a little heavily. 'Can you give me a description of him?'

'Short and fattish,' was all the girl could muster in the descriptive line.

'What was the car like?' But here again she was not very helpful.

'It was a closed car, one of them saloons.'

'And the colour?'

'It might have been black, or perhaps dark green.'

'Or red, white and blue,' growled Mr. Budd. 'What was the number?'

The girl shook her head helplessly. Regarding Marjorie she was a little more informative. 'A dark grey costume, a little black felt hat, and patent shoes.'

There was nothing more to be learned in Putney, and going back to the taxi which they had kept waiting they were driven to the Yard.

Peter was nearly frantic with anxiety, and the big detective did his best to pacify him.

'I don't think the girl will come to any harm,' he said. 'The whole object of this new idea is to use her as a basis for bargaining. They're getting scared of us, Mr. Ashton, and they want to hold Miss Arbinger as a hostage to keep us quiet. We'll be hearin' somethin' soon.'

'You don't know what they'll do,' Peter said bitterly. 'They may kill her!'

'They won't. Dead, she's no earthly use to them. Alive, she is.' He didn't add that they might do something worse, but he thought it.

Reaching the Yard, they went up to Mr. Budd's office; and within a minute of settling in the chair behind his desk, he was starting the vast organisation for inquiries which police headquarters had at its disposal. To every police station in the country went a hurried call containing descriptions of Marjorie and the car. There was a chance that this might have some effect, though Mr. Budd felt dubious. By the time the broadcast could be acted on, the girl and her captors would probably have reached their destination.

Peter felt helpless. He paced up and down Mr. Budd's bare office, smoking furiously.

'We can't do anythin' except wait,' Mr. Budd said in reply to Peter's repeated questions.

Peter telephoned an account of the kidnapping to his paper, and then waited, hoping against hope that some news would break. But no trace of the car or the girl was reported. It was twelve o'clock when he finally left to go wearily back to his flat, a tired and dispirited man.

The thought of Marjorie, helpless in the hands of the Silver Horseshoe, kept him restless and wakeful; and even when he did doze, he woke almost at once in a bath of perspiration from the nightmares which tormented him. He was up soon after five and made himself some tea. By the time he had had a bath and dressed he was feeling a little better, though his face was drawn and haggard from lack of sleep and worry.

At eight o'clock he heard the rat-tat of the post and went listlessly to collect his mail. There were three letters. Two were of no consequence, but the third, when he opened it, drove the colour from his face and brought a startled oath to his lips. It was written on cheap paper without any heading and it was from Marjorie.

'*Dear Mr. Ashton,*' it began,
    '*I am writing this at the dictation of the person responsible for my abduction this afternoon. I am unharmed at present, but unless you can comply with his demands I am not likely to remain so long. I shall not be hurt in any way if you, Mr. Bellamy, and Superintendent Budd are prepared to give up your campaign against the Silver Horseshoe. A promise to this effect in writing must be made at once and should be delivered to a messenger who will be at Holhorn tube station at eight o'clock tonight. He will wear a sprig of lavender in his button-hole. Any attempt to molest the messenger will result in my death.*
    '*The people who are holding me prisoner will release me unharmed when sufficient time has elapsed for them to complete their plans. If you*

fail to reply to this letter or should
your reply be in the negative, I shall
be maimed by the loss of one of my
fingers. I am sure they really mean
this, so please do not fail me.

'Yours sincerely,
'Marjorie Arbinger.'

Peter was round at the Yard before
Mr. Budd had put in an appearance,
and waited impatiently for him to arrive.
'I've heard from Marjorie,' he said when
the superintendent came. 'Read that!'
Mr. Budd's face set sternly as he took
in the contents. 'What can we do?' asked
the reporter. 'We must do something.
We've got to get her away from these
people.'

Mr. Budd laid the letter down on his
desk. 'How can we get her away when we
don't know where she is?' he murmured.
'This letter is written to order. It's not the
sort of letter a girl would write if she was
left to herself.'

'The meaning's the same!' said Peter
impatiently. 'Good God, maimed! We've
got to do something!'

'Well, we can't agree to what they want, anyway,' said the big man, shaking his head. 'At least I can't. Whatever happens to Miss Arbinger, Mr. Ashton, I've got to go on and try and find these people. You realise that.'

'But you can't risk them carrying out their threat! You can't!'

'I've *got* to,' said Mr. Budd. 'You and Mr. Bellamy needn't, but I've no choice.'

'Then you're going to let them do what they say?'

'Just a minute, Mr. Ashton, and let me think. We've got till eight o'clock tonight before we do anything. It all boils down to this: these people think they're playing a trump card.'

'So they are!' declared Peter. 'I'd do anything to get that girl back!'

'But we've got no guarantee that even if we agree to their demands, we should get her back. In fact, judging from the contents of the letter, it would be some time before they release her. Where was that letter posted?' He picked up the envelope. 'E.C. 4,' he said. 'That doesn't tell us anything. It's practically hopeless to try and trace the girl, in the time we've got at any rate.'

'Why not pretend to agree to what they want,' suggested Peter. 'I don't think we ought to let scruples of honour worry us. A promise extracted under threats means nothing, anyway.'

'I was considerin' that,' said the stout man, nodding. 'And you needn't worry about the honour part of it, Mr, Ashton. When I'm dealin' with people like these I don't worry about honour or anythin' like that. Yes, I think that's what we'll do. We'll draft out a letter to Miss Arbinger and we'll all sign it. See if you can get hold of Mr. Bellamy.'

Peter was at the telephone before he had finished speaking. He caught the bookmaker just as he was leaving his house for his office, and the old man was furious when he heard the news.

'The blackguards!' he said. 'I'll come straight away to the Yard, cock!'

By the time he arrived Mr. Budd had concocted a reply to Marjorie's letter, which he read to both of them. 'I think that ought to do the trick,' he said. 'It'll gain us a respite, anyway.'

Old Jacob uttered a lurid oath and clenched his huge fists. 'I'd like to 'ave five minutes alone with 'em! By the time I'd finished you could can what remained and sell it as mincemeat.'

'I'm afraid violence isn't goin' to be any use at the moment,' Mr. Budd said. 'What we've got to do is find that girl, and find her quick!'

He never took into consideration the possibility of help from the lugubrious Sergeant Leek, and yet it was that lean and melancholy man who was to discover the whereabouts of Marjorie Arbinger, and in doing so nearly bring them all to an untimely and terrible death.

13

Leek Meets with Adventure

Sergeant Leek went off to carry out his superior's instructions. He reached Peter Ashton's little cottage, deposited the bag he had brought with him containing the few essentials necessary for his toilet, and went out to survey the land.

He was certain in his own mind it was a sheer waste of time to keep a watch on Lord Sevenways. He was, however, sufficiently conscientious not to let his own predilections interfere with his duty. He discovered a point of vantage from which he could watch all exits and entrances to Broad Acres, and here he took up his stand. He caught sight of the man he was watching several times, but he only strolled about the grounds and never attempted to leave the confines of the estate. Once he was accompanied by a dark-haired woman whom Leek rightly decided was Lady Sevenways.

He spent eight long and rather boring hours at his vigil, and then he was relieved by Sergeant Eaton. He went back to the cottage, cooked himself a meal, and slept. There was an alarm clock near his head that would wake him when it was time for him to resume duty.

It woke him at half past two in the morning. He went to the sink, had a wash, and putting on his coat went out to take the place of his companion.

'Anythin' happened?' he inquired when he came upon sergeant Eaton.

'Nothing at all! The place is in darkness and everybody's asleep.'

'Wish *I* was, too,' grumbled Leek.

'Well, you've had nearly eight hours,' said his friend. 'What more d'you want?' He yawned. 'I could do with a bite of food,' he said. 'Well, so long. You've got it now till eleven and I hope you enjoy yourself.' He waved his hand and disappeared into the darkness, leaving the lean sergeant in anything but a cheerful mood. The night was a little chilly and very dark. No lights showed in any of the windows at Broad Acres, and there was nobody stirring abroad.

Leek heard a clock strike the half hour, and then, to his surprise, almost immediately after, the sound of voices. The voices were whispering, too far away for him to hear what was being said. He felt a tinge of excitement creep over him.

'Poachers, I'll bet,' he muttered to himself, and then the voices suddenly ceased. He heard the sound of approaching footsteps and drew back into the concealment of a clump of bushes in which he had taken up his position. Two figures grew dimly against the darkness

'It may be bluff.' The words came distinctly to his ears. 'I wouldn't trust them.'

'You don't suppose I have any intention of doing so, do you?' came the answer. 'That wasn't the idea at all. The idea was to get this girl Arbinger and use her as bait. We want to draw — '

The voices faded in the distance, and Leek failed to catch the end of the sentence, but he had heard enough.

He thought quickly. What should he do

— continue his watch on Broad Acres with the possibility of nothing happening, or follow the two men who had just passed him? He decided on the latter course.

Their figures were still faintly visible, dark splashes against the darker background. He crept after them. They emerged into a narrow lane that skirted the borders of Lord Sevenways's estate, and increased their pace. Leek followed warily, a little doubtful now whether he had done right. The voice of one was rough and uncultured. The other held the faintest trace of an American twang. But that mention of Arbinger was worth further inquiring into.

He held steadily to his purpose. His quarry came out of the lane onto the main thoroughfare and turned in the direction of the village. A few yards further on, two dim lights showed suddenly round the bend. As he came nearer, Leek saw that they emanated from the headlights of a standing car.

If these men had got a car he was done, helpless, unless —

An idea occurred to him. The road was bordered by a low hedge and, searching quickly, he came upon a place where it was sufficiently thin to enable him to scramble through. He tore his coat and his hands badly, but he managed it and found himself in a ploughed field. Swiftly he hurried forward. He was level with the car now; he could see the lights. It was a saloon and, by a stupendous piece of luck, there was a luggage rack attached to the back. This was what he had hoped for.

The two men were coming towards the car, and as they passed into the light of the headlamps Leek gasped. He knew the smaller — Harry Young! The man had suffered many convictions for robbery with violence. Had once been sentenced to the cat by an unsympathetic judge.

There was a gate a yard or so in front of him, and reaching this he waited. The two men came level with the car, opened the door and got in. The starter whirred and Leek, scrambling over the gate, crept silently into the roadway. The engine picked up with a rhythmic throb. Stretching out his hand, he pulled at the luggage rack until it came down, and then perched himself precariously on the grille. The car moved forward, increased its speed, and tore through the night.

Leek never forgot the discomfort of that ride. But he clung on desperately. Just before dawn, they reached London and passed through the deserted streets of the West End into the city, and on into Whitechapel Road.

They turned off the main thoroughfare and began to negotiate dark, evil-smelling streets. The tang of tarred cordage reached Leek's nostrils, and presently the lap-lap of water. He saw the bulk of moored vessels, their twinkling mast lights gleaming against the black of the sky, and presently the car stopped abruptly by a rotting wharf.

He slipped from his perch into the shadow of a warehouse. The men got out, walked to the wharf, and began to climb down what must have been a ladder. Leek waited until they had disappeared from view and then he, too, cautiously made his way to the end of the wharf, and lying flat so that he couldn't be seen, peered over the edge.

A dinghy containing his quarry was moving away; the dip-clip of its oars came plainly to his ears. His pulses beat a trifle faster. What should he do now? There was no other boat near at hand. By the time he had found one he would lose them.

There was only one thing to do, so far as he could see. Making his way down the ladder, he let himself slip gently into the water. It was icy cold, but he clenched his teeth and, guided by the faint creak of the rowlocks, struck out in the dinghy's wake.

The blackness of the night made his task of following the boat anything but an easy one, for he had to rely almost entirely on his sense of hearing. The men appeared to be keeping to the left bank of the river, hugging the moored vessels that reared their hulls out of the lapping water, and became lost in the shadows.

Leek swam with silent strokes, and presently caught a glimpse of his quarry as the rowing boat moved further out and became for an instant silhouetted against a patch of light that flickered an uneasy reflection in the water.

The boat went on downstream, the rhythmic splash of the oars plainly audible above the distant river noises. The lean sergeant followed, praying fervently that they weren't going far. Already he was numbed with the cold, and the weight of his clothes rendered swimming difficult. A tug hooted somewhere behind him and presently went past, too close to be pleasant, the wash breaking over his head. He blinked the water out of his eyes and peered ahead in search of the dinghy.

There was no sound of oars, and for a second he thought he had lost it; then dimly he made out the shadowy blot of the boat again. The rower had stopped and was evidently waiting for the tug's wash to die down.

Leek trod water and waited, too. After a minute or two the river became calm again. The rower once more bent to his oars. But this time he headed for midstream, and it soon became clear to the sergeant that he was making for the opposite bank.

Leek altered his course. By the time he had reached the middle of the river he became aware that there were treacherous cross-currents. It was as though some hidden monster with many tentacles was pulling his legs; his arms ached, and his whole body cried out in sympathy with them, when he eventually succeeded in crossing the broad waterway.

The boat with the two men had pulled in under the shadow of a barge that lay moored to a buoy. Hanging on to the slimy pile of a wharf, panting and nearly exhausted, Leek watched them secure the dinghy to a trailing rope and swarm up another onto the deck.

In spite of his physical discomfort, he felt a thrill of excitement tingle his pulses. Was his decision to follow the men who had passed him near Broad Acres going to bear fruit? Possibly he had discovered the whereabouts of the girl. In his mind's eye he pictured his dramatic appearance at Scotland Yard and his report to Mr. Budd.

Slowly he swam in the direction of the dark bulk of the barge into whose shadows the men had vanished. He reached it eventually and, grasping the gunwale of the dinghy, pulled himself aboard and began to massage his cramped and numbed limbs. In a little while he had partially restored the circulation and started to consider his next move.

Obviously the first thing to do was to explore the barge, and so cautiously and without noise he began to climb up the dangling knotted rope hand over hand. A few seconds later he was standing on the deck.

Looking round, he saw that there was a low cabin amid-ships from the side of which a dull gleam of light shone. On tiptoe, fearful that the flop-flop of his sodden shoes would be heard, he made his way over to this dim splash of radiance. It came from an oblong window almost flush with the deck.

Stretching himself full length, the sergeant peered in through the dirty glass. He was able to see dimly a table, over which swung an oil lamp. On the table stood a bottle of whisky, and sitting facing him was Harry Young. He was talking to the other man, who was perched on the edge of the table.

Leek watched eagerly. He could hear nothing of what was being said, and he wondered what he should do next. As he moved with the intention of rising to his feet, a hand gripped him by the collar and jerked him up.

'Now then,' greeted a harsh voice, 'what the hell do you think you're doing?' Leek twisted his head. The grip was so tight that it was almost choking him. 'Come on, answer!' snarled his captor, shaking him violently. 'Who the devil are you? And what are you doing spying about this barge?'

The sergeant decided to bluff. Letting his muscles go limp, he allowed himself to hang flabbily in the other's grasp.

'I ain't doin' nothing,' he whined nasally. 'You let me go, guv'nor. I just fell into the river,' went on Leek, searching his brain for a feasible story. 'Was looking for some place to doss and fell off the wharf in the dark.'

The grasp on his collar relaxed. 'Well,' grunted the other, 'you'd better fall into the river again. We don't want you here.'

251

He gave the sergeant a push and sent him staggering up against the cabin.

The voices had evidently reached the ears of the two men inside, for the door opened and a stream of light cut into the darkness.

'What's all this row?' asked someone sharply. 'Are you mad or drunk?'

'Neither! I found this feller spying into the cabin.'

'Who is he?' said a voice sharply.

'Here he is.' The man caught Leek by the arm and swung him round into the light. 'Says he fell into the river while he was looking for somewhere to sleep. Best thing is to throw him back.'

'Throw him back nothing,' replied a voice, and the taller man he had seen with Harry Young peered at him intently. 'I've seen this fellow somewhere. Take him down into the cabin where I can see him properly.'

They hauled Leek down the steps and flung him on the floor of the cabin.

'He's a busy!' snarled Harry Young. 'I know 'im. 'e got me a stretch once. He's a feller called Leek.'

14

The Lavender Man

Peter Ashton's imagination conjured up all kinds of terrible things that might be happening to Marjorie Arbinger, and in consequence he was irritable and inclined to be snappy. Mr. Budd heaved a sigh of relief when old Jacob Bellamy succeeded at last in persuading the reporter to go out with him for lunch.

The superintendent had laid his plans, as far as he could. It had been decided that Ashton should deliver the letter to the messenger of the Silver Horseshoe who would be waiting at Holborn tube station at eight that night. Mr. Budd and Jacob Bellamy, in a closed car, would wait nearby and trail the 'lavender man', as Mr. Budd dubbed him, to his destination. There was a possible chance that he might lead them to Marjorie Arbinger, or at any rate to someone who could supply a clue to the girl's whereabouts.

Throughout the rest of the afternoon he sat in his padded chair. No report had as yet come in from Leek, and although he had scarcely expected any he was a little disappointed. Sergeant Eaton had been dispatched that morning with instructions to relieve the melancholy man, and to telephone immediately should there be anything to report.

At five o'clock Mr. Budd roused himself and went out to the tea shop round the corner. In an hour he was back and resumed his position behind the desk.

At seven Peter and Jacob Bellamy returned. 'We'd better make a start, hadn't we?' said Peter, looking more haggard than ever.

'In a quarter of an hour,' answered Mr. Budd. 'That'll be plenty of time, Mr. Ashton.'

'We've got to be careful, cock,' said old Jacob. 'If this feller gets it into his head he's being followed, it may bring trouble on that girl.'

'We've *got* to take the risk!' said Mr.

Budd slowly. 'Miss Arbinger's got to be found, and quickly, and that's the only way I can think of to find her.'

At a quarter past seven he put on his hat and coat and went down, followed by his two companions, to where a car was waiting in the courtyard. Mr. Budd climbed in and squeezed behind the wheel. 'I'm goin' to drop you off some distance away from the meetin' place, Mr. Ashton, and we'll pick you up after.'

They came out of the arch into Whitehall, crossed Trafalgar Square and sped along the Strand towards the Aldwych. It was twenty to eight when Mr. Budd slowed down and brought the car to a halt in Kingsway. 'Slip out,' he said to Peter, without turning his head, and the reporter obeyed.

The big man sent the car forward again, stopping it presently at a place where he could command a view of the tube station. Here he waited. After an interval Peter arrived, bought an evening paper from a news-seller, and took up his stand, scanning the printed sheets.

It was eight o'clock precisely when they caught their first glimpse of the messenger. He came from the direction of Southampton Row, walking quickly — a tallish, shabbily dressed man wearing in the lapel of his overcoat a sprig of lavender.

Reaching the main entrance of the station he stopped, glanced quickly about him, and lighted a cigarette. The watchful Mr. Budd saw that Peter had already seen him. The reporter closed his paper and strolled towards the man. He said something and the other nodded. Peter put his hand in his pocket and produced the envelope containing the letter which they had concocted that morning. The other took it, stowed it away inside his shabby coat, and with a curt nod made off down Kingsway.

Mr. Budd started his engine and slowly turned the car. As he came snailing along the sidewalk Peter stepped forward, opened the door, and sprang in.

'What did he say?' grunted Mr. Budd, his eyes still watching the receding figure of the messenger.

'Nothing!' grunted the reporter. 'He took the letter and went off.'

'He doesn't seem to be afraid of being followed,' muttered Bellamy. 'He hasn't looked round once.'

They moved slowly in the wake of the hurrying figure, keeping fifty yards in the rear. At Aldwych the man boarded a city-going bus, and Mr. Budd blessed the forethought that had provided them with a car. At Ludgate Circus their quarry descended and picked up another bus bound for Aldgate.

'Goin' to the East End,' murmured Mr. Budd.

The man got down at Aldgate station and began to walk quickly along towards Whitechapel. The pavements were crowded and they had some difficulty keeping him in sight. The bright lights of a public house came in sight and the man hesitated, turned, and passed through the swing doors of the saloon bar. The superintendent brought the car to a stop. 'How long's he goin' to stop here?' he muttered.

'Is there likely to be another exit?' said

Peter anxiously. 'We don't want him to give us the slip.'

'I was wondering that,' said the big man. 'You take charge of the car, Mr. Ashton, and I'll have a look round.'

The Feathers was built on the corner of a side turning, and Mr. Budd took stock of it carefully. So far as he could see, there was no way by which the quarry could give them the slip, and he came back to the car. He had barely done so before the man reappeared and continued his way along the Whitechapel Road.

As Mr. Budd squeezed himself in beside Peter, they saw the man turn off into a side street.

'Listen,' said Mr. Budd, 'it's no good taking the car down there. We'd better park it somewhere and follow on foot.'

'There's a garage on the opposite side of the road,' said Peter. 'You and Jacob keep an eye on the man while I run the car over.'

Mr. Budd got out, followed by Bellamy. Peter accelerated, swung the machine round, and ran it into the convenient garage. By the time he returned there was no sign of his two companions, but halfway down the narrow side street he met them.

'He's gone into one of those houses,' whispered Mr. Budd, nodding towards the gloomy buildings with which the narrow street was lined.

'D'you think that's where they've got Marjorie?' asked the reporter.

'I should doubt it, Mr. Ashton,' Mr Budd answered. 'These are ordinary lodging houses by the look of them. Maybe where this fellow lives.'

Ten o'clock came and went. Eleven ... Twelve ...

It appeared that the 'lavender man' was going to stop there all night, for there was no sign of his reappearance. They were cold and weary from their vigil and disappointed at the result. At half past one they held a conference.

'I don't see why you two should lose a night's sleep,' said the superintendent. 'You and Mr. Bellamy get off home, Mr. Ashton. I'll stay and keep an eye on this fellow.'

But the others protested. If anything

was going to happen they were going to be in it.

The hours passed slowly, and then at half past four they heard a slight sound: the gentle thud of a closing door. It brought them to alert watchfulness. A figure came out of the narrow entrance of the house into which the 'lavender man' had vanished, and as it passed into the dim radiance of the street lamp they saw it was their quarry. He slunk off rapidly down the street, in the opposite direction to the main road, and the three weary watchers followed.

They had proceeded some distance when a feel of dampness in the air warned them of the proximity of the river. 'He's making for the riverside,' murmured Mr. Budd as they plunged into a narrow opening between the shadowy bulk of two warehouses. 'We'll have to be careful or we'll be losin' him.'

His warning was justified. In coming out of the alley, they discovered that their quarry had given them the slip. There was no sign of him anywhere.

'Stand still a minute and listen,' said

the big man, and although they followed his advice they could hear nothing.

'He must have gone down one of those two turnings,' said Peter. 'There's no other exit from this street; it's a cul-de-sac.'

'Come on then,' said Mr. Budd. 'Maybe we'll be lucky and pick him up again.'

They went down the first of the narrow alleys. It brought them eventually to a strip of wharfage, but it was deserted.

Mr. Budd's searching eyes espied a dim object pulled up in the shadow of a building. He moved over towards it, followed by the others, and discovered it was an empty car. He touched the radiator and found it unpleasantly warm.

'Queer,' he muttered. 'Now, I wonder if . . .' He broke off and stared across the gloomy expanse of dark water, trying to pierce the blackness. A sound had reached his ears — the sound of voices from somewhere in the darkness. 'Listen!' he whispered.

They heard a muffled altercation, and

then the unmistakable sound of a struggle.

'I ain't doin' nothin'!' came a whining voice distinctly. 'You let me go, guv'nor!'

Mr. Budd started and his jaw dropped, for he had recognised the voice as belonging to Sergeant Leek.

* * *

The three men glared down into the upturned face of the unfortunate sergeant, and the man who called himself Stanmore nodded. 'So that's who he is, is he?' he remarked softly.

'I tell yer,' said Leek, 'I was lookin' for somewhere to kip, an' fell in the water.'

'Keep quiet!' ordered Stanmore. 'Get some rope and tie him up,' he went on to his two companions. 'And gag him. Was he following you, Marks?'

The man with the sprig of lavender in his coat shook his head. 'No, he wasn't following me, Boss,' he answered. 'He was here when I arrived, crouching down by the cabin window.'

'H'm!' Stanmore frowned. 'I wonder

how he got here? What about the others?'

'They're here all right.' Marks grinned. 'Followed me from the tube station. Thought I didn't see 'em, but I did. I give the perishers a good wait, anyhow! Left 'em watching while I went into me digs and had a sleep.'

'All three of them, eh?' said Stanmore.

'That's right!' said Marks. 'I shouldn't be surprised if we didn't see something of 'em before long.'

'Tracey'll attend to them,' said the tall man. 'Did you get the letter?'

'Yes,' replied the other. 'The reporter feller brought it. Here y'are.' He put his hand into his pocket and pulled out the envelope which Peter had given him at Holborn. Mr. Stanmore ripped it open, read the contents, and tossed it aside contemptuously.

'Do they take us for children?' he sneered. 'I guess they're under the impression we're going to believe this.'

'You're taking a bit of a risk, ain't yer?' Marks said.

'No! You should use your brains more,' snapped Stanmore. 'They did exactly what I expected them to do — followed you, under the impression that we'd believe this letter and that they'd agreed to our terms. It's what's known as a double-bluff. You got that fellow tied up?' He turned to the man who had accompanied him from the neighbourhood of Broad Acres.

'Yes, and he'll be clever if he can wriggle out of it,' was the reply.

'Shove him over there,' said Stanmore, 'and then come up on deck. I think we shall have some visitors in a minute or two, and I'd like to give them a good welcome!'

* * *

Mr. Budd turned a wondering face towards Peter. 'That was Leek!' he declared. 'I'd know his voice anywhere.'

'It can't be,' said the reporter. 'I thought you sent Leek down to my cottage.'

'I did, but he ain't there now. He's somewhere out here, and I think he's in trouble.' He moved away towards the edge of the wharf and began peering about in the darkness.

'What are you lookin' for, cock?' said Bellamy below his breath.

'A boat,' answered Mr. Budd. 'I want to find out what's happening.'

Eventually it was Peter who discovered a battered dinghy moored to a crazy landing stage several yards further along. He reported his discovery and Mr. Budd turned to Bellamy. 'Can you row, Mr. Bellamy?' he inquired, and when the bookmaker nodded: 'That's good, because I can't!'

'I can, anyway,' said Peter, 'and I'm younger than Jacob.'

'It's no good the three of us going in case there's any trouble,' Mr. Budd said. 'Mr. Bellamy and I will go, and you can pop along to the nearest police station. Tell 'em to put a call through to the information room at Scotland Yard, mentionin' my name, and askin' that all squad cars in the vicinity should be wirelessed to meet at this place. Find out the name of that road we came down as you go back.'

Peter agreed, somewhat reluctantly.

The superintendent climbed down into the boat, followed by Jacob Bellamy. Luckily there was a pair of sculls stowed away under one of the seats, and these the bookmaker pulled out and thrust into the rowlocks.

The scuffling noise had ceased, but the big man had marked the direction from which it had come, and Bellamy sent the dinghy dancing over the water with long, powerful strokes. Presently they came in sight of a line of moored barges, and then, a few feet away, the dark bulk of another tied up to a buoy by itself. A light shone dimly and Mr. Budd tapped the bookmaker gently on the shoulder.

'Make for that one where the light is,' he whispered.

The old man obeyed, and presently the dinghy came under the shadow of the clumsy boat.

'There's another boat moored here,' said Mr. Budd, with his lips close to his companion's ear. 'Be careful; don't let her bump.'

He fended off the prow of the dinghy,

and his hand came in contact with a rope and held on as Bellamy softly shipped the sculls. The gentle swell of the river moved them up and down, lapping round the little boat, but there was no other sound. If Leek was aboard this barge he was keeping very quiet, or something had happened to him.

The superintendent looked at the rope to which he was holding and frowned. He wanted very much to climb on board, but he knew that to swarm up that rope was beyond him.

'I think I could manage it, cock,' said Bellamy, when Mr. Budd whispered his difficulty. 'Then I can haul you up after me.'

'For the lord's sake, don't make a noise!' said the big man.

The darkness had given place to a faint grey, a herald of the coming dawn, sufficient to enable them to see a little clearer.

Old Jacob grasped the rope and began to pull himself up. Mr. Budd watched him admiringly. He went slowly but surely, and presently scrambled over the low gunwale onto the deck. The stout Superintendent saw him lean down and stretch out his hands.

Standing up gingerly in the bobbing little boat, he grasped them, felt himself drawn up, and for a moment hung precariously against the smooth side of the barge. The next moment he was beside Bellamy. The old man was panting heavily.

'Didn't think I could manage it,' he whispered triumphantly. 'Well, here we are.'

'Here you are, gentlemen!' said a voice. 'Put up your hands, please. And keep 'em up! There are three automatics covering you. At the slightest movement you'll be shot dead!'

Mr. Budd could dimly make out the three shadowy forms that had emerged from behind the low structure of the cabin. 'Good mornin'. I suppose you're part of this Horseshoe outfit?'

'Correct!' said the man called Stanmore. 'We were expecting you.'

'I see,' said the big man. 'Well, what now? You can't hold us up like this for ever.'

'I don't intend to!' Stanmore retorted. 'There's a cabin downstairs; you'll be safe enough there.' He made a gesture towards the opening. 'Go on, down you go!' he snapped. 'Try anything funny and it'll be the last thing you do!'

It was useless arguing, and Mr. Budd obeyed. The first thing he saw as he entered the dimly lighted cabin was the bound figure of Leek. He had expected to see the girl but there was no sign of her.

Stanmore came down the steps behind them. 'Just one more and the party is complete. Tie 'em up, Young.'

Harry Young advanced, an unpleasant grin on his face, and Mr. Budd raised his eyebrows. 'So you're in this racket, are you?' he murmured. 'Well, it looks as if you'll go down for another stretch, Harry. You had the 'cat' last time, didn't you?'

'You keep your mouth shut!' growled the man angrily. He picked up a length of rope and three minutes later both the superintendent and the bookmaker were as helpless as Leek.

'Now we shan't need these anymore,' said Stanmore, pocketing his automatic and signing to the other two to do the same. 'You're quite — ' He broke off as a low whistle came from outside. 'That's Tracey,' he said, turning to Harry Young. 'Go and help him, will you.'

The man hurried up the steps and disappeared, to return presently with another man, carrying between them a limp form which they laid on the cabin floor.

Mr. Budd saw the white face in the light of the lamp and his heart sank. It was Peter Ashton!

15

A Matter of Seconds

'Good! Now everything's complete!' said Stanmore. 'We'll have to get a move on. You were later, Marks, than I'd reckoned.'

'Me alarm clock let me down,' said the man with a sprig of lavender in his coat.

'Never mind.' The tall man waved the explanation aside impatiently. 'You and Young fetch the girl and take her ashore. Tracey and I will attend to these.'

The two men nodded and disappeared.

'Bind that fellow and gag the others,' ordered Stanmore, and Tracey carried out his instructions.

'What are you going to do with them?' he asked. 'Croak 'em?'

'You've guessed it in one!' Stanmore answered easily. He came over and stood looking down at Mr. Budd. 'In a few minutes we shall be leaving this barge for good. But you and your two friends'll stay behind — also for good. I've no more use either for you or the barge, and you may as well go together.'

Tracey looked puzzled. 'What are you going to do?' he asked doubtfully. 'You ain't going to leave 'em here alive, are you?'

'I shall *leave* them here alive,' replied the man called Stanmore significantly, 'but I can assure you they won't be alive very long. It's practically high tide, or will be in a few minutes. Just before we go we shall remove the bilge-plugs. It should take about half an hour for this old tub to fill, and when it finally settles in the mud at the bottom of the river its stateroom will contain passengers.'

'I see!' said Tracey. 'Going to sink the barge and drown 'em, eh?'

'That's the idea. Now let's scram!' Stanmore gave a quick glance round, picked up a glass half-full of whisky, and drained it. 'You thought you were being very clever,' he said, 'when you followed Marks, but I guessed what you'd do, and I had Tracey following you. He was watching all the time. He heard you give instructions for Ashton to notify the police, and he put a stop to that. I guessed what you'd do, took a chance on you doing it, and won!'

Mr. Budd felt his heart sink. Bound hand and foot and unable to move, they would be drowned like rats in a sewer — dead long before the old barge finally vanished for good beneath the swirling waters of the river. It would be a horrible death.

There came the sound of shuffling feet on deck outside and Stanmore went over to the cabin door. 'They're getting the girl away,' he said, and Tracey looked surprised.

'Ain't she going down with this lot?' he inquired.

'No!' the tall man snapped curtly. 'Get along to the boat. I'll join you in a second.' Tracey shrugged, mounted the steps, and disappeared.

Stanmore came over, tested the cords that bound them all, and then without a word went out too. The key clicked in the lock.

For a long time there was silence, and

then faintly to their ears came the sound of gurgling water. The bilge plugs had been removed. Footsteps thudded on the deck, followed after a short interval by the creaking of oars, and then silence once more.

From somewhere in the distance came the faint hoot of a siren. The swinging lamp which had been growing dimmer flickered, turned blue for a moment or two, flared up with a last spurt of energy, and went out, leaving the four helpless men to face the rising of the waters in darkness.

Tightly bound hand and foot, Mr. Budd stared into the blackness, concentrating every atom of his intelligence on trying to evolve some means of escaping from this terrible predicament. He could hear the sounds of his companion's breathing and an occasional weird noise as Bellamy and Lock tried vainly to eject the gags which had been skilfully bound round their mouths.

How long had they got? he wondered. At the moment there was no sign of the water he could hear gushing through the bilge-plugs, but it wouldn't be long before it entered the cabin and slowly rose, inch by inch.

Mr. Budd had repeatedly tried to raise himself into a sitting posture, hoping by this means to put off the seemingly inevitable by a few minutes. But he soon discovered that this was physically impossible. Breathless from his exertions, he relaxed for a second — and suddenly felt a cold, clammy touch stealing beneath his body.

The water had already entered the cabin! The floor was wet to his fingers!

At that rate it would be less than fifteen minutes before it rose high enough to cover his mouth and nostrils, and then . . . He shuddered. Death was very near, and there seemed no hope; no hope either for himself or for his three companions!

To die like this, caged up and drowned like so much vermin, was horrible. It worried him, too, that he had brought Bellamy and Peter Ashton into the trouble with him. He should never have allowed them to overrule his first insistence that they should keep out of it.

This sort of risk was part of his job — part of Leek's, too, for that matter. But Bellamy . . .

The water was lapping his chin. Well, it wouldn't last much longer now. The sooner it was over the better.

He had to keep his mouth closed and breathe through his nostrils. Another minute at the most would see the end!

He heard a movement beside him and a grunt. What was happening to the others? Peter had been unconscious. Had he recovered or had he succumbed without? Perhaps that would be best . . .

But his stubbornness and tenacity made him try to ward off death until the last possible moment. With a considerable amount of trouble and no little pain, he managed to twist himself onto his knees and knelt precariously, swaying backwards and forwards. His hands, bound to his ankles, forced him to bend his large body back in a bow. It was difficult to keep his balance and also to breathe, but it would give him a short respite.

His back was aching violently. He felt his senses swimming. And then suddenly there came a sound, and the shock of it restored his mental alertness.

It was a stealthy step on the deck above!

For a moment he thought he was suffering from hallucinations, and then he heard it again louder. A moment later the latch of the cabin door was rattled vigorously.

'Anyone there?' called a voice.

Mr. Budd tried vainly to reply, but he only achieved a hoarse rattle in his throat. The gag of cotton waste choked back all intelligible sounds.

There came a tremendous thud on the door, followed by another; and then, with a splintering crash, it gave way. The light of an electric torch spread fan-like, wavered through the darkness, and came to rest on the figure of Mr. Budd.

Someone behind the light uttered an exclamation, and then came splashing through the water towards him. The gag was torn from his mouth and an arm supported him.

'I guess I'm only just in time!' said a familiar voice, and the stout man recognised the nasal accents of Mr. Piggott!

The torch was set down on a ledge and the American produced a clasp knife, which he opened quickly and slashed through the ropes.

As he helped Mr. Budd to his feet, the big man found his voice. 'I'm all right,' he gasped hoarsely. 'Look after them other three.'

Piggott obeyed. Stooping, he hauled Peter Ashton up and lifted him onto the table. 'Here, you free him,' he said, handing his knife to the superintendent, and turned his attention to Leek and Bellamy. In a few minutes they were all free.

'How did you get here?' demanded the detective, eyeing his rescuer.

'Never mind that!' answered the American. 'I guess that'll wait. We've got to look slippy and get off before this old hulk goes down.'

Peter had recovered consciousness, but he was still shaky, and they had to help him between them up the steps and onto the sloping deck. The barge had already developed a list, which in a way proved providential, for there was less distance between its deck and the boat that had brought Mr. Piggott.

They lifted Peter, dropped him into the swaying dinghy, and followed one by one. The American was the last to take his place, and as the little boat moved away from the sinking barge, Mr. Budd uttered a sigh of thankfulness.

'Well, that's the nearest shave I ever want to see!' he declared.

'The swine!' growled Jacob Bellamy, rubbing his numbed limbs. 'I'd just like to have that thin feller all to meself for ten minutes!'

The dazed Peter, shivering with cold, looked from one to the other. 'Where's Marjorie?' he whispered huskily. 'They've still got her.'

'Now that's where you're wrong, Mr. Ashton!' said the American. 'Miss Arbinger's quite safe and sound.'

'Where is she?' demanded the reporter.

'In my car,' said Mr. Piggott with a chuckle. 'In a moment or two you'll be seeing her.'

* * *

The proprietor of the Pewter Pot, that resort of seafaring men in Whitechapel Road, received the biggest surprise of his life when at half past six he was called to receive five men and a girl in the dingy vestibule of his unpretentious establishment.

'We want a private room, a fire, and some hot coffee,' said Mr. Piggott curtly. 'And we want it quick!'

'I'm afraid I can't allow the lady in, sir,' said Mr. Smith, glancing doubtfully at his visitors and noting that four of the male members were soaked to the skin.

'Now look here, Slogger,' growled a voice, 'just do as you're told, and don't let's have any nonsense!'

Slogger Smith turned towards the speaker and his face changed.

'Blimey, it's Jacob Bellamy! Well, I'll be — I ain't seen you for years, Jacob!' Mr. Smith became suddenly galvanised into action. 'Hi! Marty!' he roared. 'Put a fire in number four, and get some coffee. Look slippy now!'

A ginger-haired, cadaverous man dressed in trousers and a singlet, who had been looking on suspiciously, gave a nod and hurried away.

'I didn't know it was you, Mr. Bellamy,' apologised the proprietor. 'Of course you and any of your friends are welcome. If you takes my advice you'll have a drop of something stronger than coffee. How about a tot of rum?'

'The very thing!' said the bookmaker. 'Bring us some, Slogger.' Mr. Smith disappeared through a door that led to the bar.

'Is there anybody you *don't* know, Jacob?' remarked Peter through chattering teeth.

'Very few,' growled the old man. 'Slogger used to be one of the best amateur 'eavy weights of 'is time. Remember my knockin' you out at Charlie Gill's place?' he went on as Mr. Smith returned with a tray containing a black bottle and glasses.

'It took you all your time, though, Jacob, didn't it?' he answered, grinning. 'And it'd take you all your time now. I still 'ave a spar with one or two of the boys.' Deftly he filled the glasses with the spirit. 'What about the young lady?'

'I'll wait for the coffee,' said Marjorie.

'That's the best drop of rum you can get anywhere,' said Slogger Smith.

'And tastes all the better,' said Mr. Bellamy as he swallowed his portion at a gulp, 'for havin' had no duty paid on it!'

Mr. Smith uttered a protest.

Mr. Budd was prepared to agree with Bellamy. The spirit had driven out the unpleasant chill which had crept into his bones.

The ginger-haired man appeared at that moment to inform them that the fire was alight, and the proprietor led them up a flight of stairs to a long corridor from which several rooms opened. At the door of one of these he stopped and ushered them into a plain, barely furnished room, in the grate of which a fire crackled merrily. 'Now I'll go and see about your coffee,' he said. 'I won't be two shakes!'

He disappeared, closing the door behind him. They pulled up the truckle bed in front of the fireplace and sat down.

'Why haven't you drunk your rum?' asked Mr. Budd, looking at Leek severely.

'I never drink nothin' alcoholic, you know that.'

'You'll drink that,' said the big man impatiently. 'It's medicine! Otherwise we'll have you on the sick list.'

The sergeant, looking more melancholy and miserable than usual, raised the glass to his lips.

'It won't poison you!' said Mr. Budd, as Leek made a wry face. 'Swallow it quickly!'

Leek obeyed, then choked, and broke into a violent fit of coughing. 'Oh!' he gasped weakly, blinking the tears out of his eyes. 'It's burnin' me throat!'

'Nonsense!' snapped the superintendent unsympathetically. He turned to the smiling Mr. Piggott. 'Now, sir, I should like you to do a little explainin'. F'instance, how is it you always manage to turn up when there's trouble about?'

'Call it instinct,' said Mr. Piggott blandly.

'I can call it a lot of things,' grunted the

big man significantly. 'How did you manage to be on the spot in time to get us out of that death trap?'

'Never look a gift horse in the mouth,' said Mr. Piggott.

'Meanin' that you're not talkin'?' said Mr. Budd.

'Yes,' agreed Mr. Piggott, nodding gently. 'I was there, luckily for you, and that's sufficient.'

'It's not sufficient for me,' murmured the superintendent. 'But perhaps you won't mind tellin' us how you managed to rescue Miss Arbinger?'

'No, I don't mind that,' said Mr. Piggott generously. 'I saw those fellows bring Miss Arbinger ashore and put her in a car. They went back to the wharf for something or other, and while they were gone I slipped along and carried the lady to my own car, which I'd hidden in a side turning a little distance away.' He chuckled softly. 'You've never seen anyone so astonished as those guys were when they came back and found she'd gone.'

'H'm!' said Mr. Budd. 'Now let's hear your story, Leek. How did you come to be on that barge, when I thought you was watchin' Lord Sevenways?'

'I saw two fellers,' said the sergeant a little thickly. 'I 'eard 'em make some remark about Miss Arbinger.' He explained at length, and they listened interestedly.

'So they came from Sevenways's house, did they?' grunted Mr. Budd.

'I don't know,' answered Leek, 'but they came from near abouts.'

'You said somethin' about Sevenways bein' at the bottom of this business after that schermozzle at Mr. Ashton's cottage,' Mr. Budd remarked, looking at the American. 'Now what did you mean?'

'I didn't say he was at the bottom of it; I said he was *responsible* for it,' corrected Mr. Piggott.

'Well, it's the same thing,' grunted Mr. Budd.

'No, it's not! Lord Sevenways *is* responsible for the Silver Horseshoe, but I don't suppose he knows anything about it.'

The stout man sighed wearily. 'It'd be a good thing if some people'd speak plainly,' he remarked.

The ginger-haired waiter brought the coffee at that moment and nothing more was said until he had taken his departure.

'You seem to know a lot about this Horseshoe business,' said old Jacob Bellamy, frowning at the smiling Mr. Piggott.

'Yes,' agreed the American. 'Or perhaps I should say I *guess* a little about it.'

'If I did my duty I ought to arrest you,' Mr. Budd remarked.

'It wouldn't do you any good,' said Mr. Piggott amiably. 'I haven't done a single thing against the law.'

'You're withholdin' information that might lead to the capture of a dangerous organisation,' snapped Mr. Budd. 'And that's an offence!'

'There's a deal of difference between guessing and knowing, and what I *think* isn't evidence.' retorted Mr. Piggott

Mr. Budd knew he was right. 'Well,' he said, after a tremendous gulp of the hot coffee which Marjorie had poured out, 'you're not a detective by any chance, are you?'

'No, sir! I am *not* a detective.'

'Of course he isn't!' said Leek suddenly and unexpectedly. 'There's only one detective in the 'ole world — an' that's me! I'm the greatest detective that ever lived!' he went on extravagantly, while the others stared at him in blank astonishment. 'I ought to be a sup'rintendent!'

'You ought to be in a home!' snarled Mr. Budd.

Leek glared at him. 'You might be a good detective, too, if you weren't so fat!'

'What!' gasped the superintendent.

'You 'eard!' The thin sergeant wagged an admonishing finger at him. 'You've got fatty de-de-degeneration of the brain! That's what's the matter with you!'

'He's tight!' whispered Peter Ashton in amazement.

'Leek, behave yourself!' snapped Mr. Budd angrily.

'You shut up!' said the sergeant offensively. 'Now I'm goin' to talk fer a change.' He blinked at them malignantly. 'I've got somethin' to talk about. The greatest detective the world 'as ever seen! Thass me! Ebenezer Leek!'

'Pull yourself together!' snarled the superintendent. 'And don't behave like a lunatic.'

'Don't you go callin' me names!' said the sergeant, rising unsteadily to his feet. 'The greatest detective what was ever born! Let me tell you I've come of an old, 'ard-livin' family. The fightin' Leeks! Thass what we was called!'

Peter burst out laughing.

'You lie down for a bit,' advised Mr. Budd. 'It's the rum, that's what it is.'

'Nonshense!' said the sergeant with difficulty. 'Alcohol has no effect. I could drink all of you under the table!' He staggered as he spoke and clutched the back of a chair, surveying them glassily.

'You'll be under the table yourself in a minute!' said the superintendent. 'Sit down, and don't make an idiot of yourself!'

Leek sat down abruptly as Mr. Budd gave him a gentle push. 'Now,' said the superintendent. 'You dry up! D'you hear?'

The sergeant muttered, ' . . . greatest detective,' and subsided into a stupor.

'We'd better get him home,' said Mr.

Budd. 'It was my fault. I ought never to have let him drink that rum.'

'I think,' suggested Mr. Piggott, 'we'd better go. There seems no sense in hanging about here, and it wouldn't do any harm to you people to get into dry clothes as soon as possible. The rum and the coffee and the fire will have prevented a chill, but you ought to get those wet things off as soon as you can.'

There was sense in his words, and they agreed. Old Jacob Bellamy called Slogger Smith and settled the bill, in spite of that gentleman's protestations.

Marty was sent to secure a taxi, since Mr. Piggott's car was not big enough to hold them all. When this, after some difficulty, had been found and the now-semiconscious Leek deposited in it, they drove to the garage where Peter had left the police car, Mr. Piggott having elected to drive Marjorie Arbinger to her home.

Leek was deposited at his lodgings in Kensington, with a word of explanation to his astonished and scandalized land-lady; and when Mr. Budd had been dropped at his Streatham villa, Peter drove back to his flat for a bath and a change.

It freshened him up a little, although there was a lot of work to be done before he could legitimately claim the rest his soul craved.

At twelve o'clock he was in the reporters' room at the *Morning Mail* typing furiously, and the account of the night's happenings which he presently took along to Mr. Sorbet brought joy to the eyes of even that usually pessimistic and disillusioned man.

16

The Cablegram

Refreshed by a bath, a change of clothes, and a good meal, Mr. Budd put in an appearance at Scotland Yard shortly after two. There was a long cablegram awaiting him on his desk and he read it slowly, with ever-increasing astonishment.

It was an answer to the one he had dispatched to America, and it contained sufficient surprising information to give him much food for thought; for here was a definite clue to the identity of the persons behind the activities of the Silver Horseshoe, and the mystery which lay behind those activities.

From the start Mr. Budd had had a hunch that there was something deeper than the ordinary racket which appeared on the surface, and what he had now learned tended to confirm this theory. He read the cablegram again, folded it carefully, put it in his pocket, and lit one of his atrocious cigars. With half-closed eyes, his hands clasped lightly across his capacious stomach, he smoked his cigar through to the end; and then, getting up leisurely, he left his cheerless room and made his way to the Aliens' Department.

The genial, grey-haired Inspector Labbet welcomed him. 'Come in, sir,' he said. 'What are you after this time?' Mr. Budd told him, and the other whistled.

'I know the man you mean,' he said. 'But he isn't in this country — not unless he's slipped in without our knowing it, which'd be a very difficult thing to do.'

'I'll bet you any money you like, Labbet, he's in this country now, and making himself felt!'

The head of the Aliens' Department eyed him shrewdly. 'He's connected with this Silver Horseshoe, I suppose you mean?' he hazarded, and the big man nodded.

'You think the 'Kid's' running it?' asked the inspector. 'Well, I shouldn't be surprised.'

'I should!' asserted Mr. Budd. 'No, I

don't think he's runnin' it, Labbet, but I think he's got a lot to do with it. I wouldn't like to tell you who *I* think's runnin' it, because you'd have a fit. So would a lot of people! There's another thing I want you to do. I want you to trace up a man who calls himself Samuel K. Piggott. Find out all about him. I'll give you his present address.' He pulled a sheet of paper towards him and scribbled it down. 'There y'are. Get on to him and cable his description to New York and ask 'em if they can give any information about him.'

'Is he in the Horseshoe business, too?' demanded Labbet, as he made a note of his superior's requirements.

'I don't know what he's in,' answered Mr. Budd candidly. 'But he knows far too much to please me, and I'd like to know a little more about him.'

'I'll do my best,' said the inspector, and the stout man returned to his office. Sergeant Leek was sitting dejectedly on the only other chair the room contained.

'Oh!' said Mr. Budd severely. 'So you've recovered, have you?'

'I've still got a bit of an 'ead,' said the sergeant lugubriously.

'You're lucky you've got nothin' worse,' said his superior. 'I suppose you know that I ought to report you for insubordination?'

'Did I disgrace meself?' asked Leek plaintively.

Mr. Budd eyed him witheringly. 'I've never seen such an exhibition in me life!'

'Well, you shouldn't 'ave made me drink the stuff,' protested the aggrieved sergeant. 'What 'appened?'

'I don't think we'd better discuss it,' said Mr. Budd with dignity. He squeezed himself into his padded chair and lolled back. 'When my own sergeant informs me that I'd make a good detective if I wasn't so fat, it's better relegated to the limbo of forgotten things!'

'Did I say that?' whispered the horrified Leek.

'Among other things,' said the superintendent. 'I'm not surprised you've got an 'eadache. It swelled so large that I wonder you've got any 'ead at all! It ought to have bust!'

'If I said anythin' like you say I said,' muttered, the sergeant almost tearfully, 'I didn't mean it. I wouldn't 'ave said it, not if it 'adn't been for the rum. You know that!'

'You must have been 'arbourin' these thoughts, though,' answered his superior. 'Fat I may be, but I'm not fat-headed like some people I know.' He allowed this to sink in, and then continued: 'Sergeant Eaton has been on the telephone, wonderin' what the deuce has happened to you. As I wasn't here nobody could tell him. You'd better cut off back to Broad Acres.'

'You still want me to keep an eye on his lordship?' asked Leek, a little relieved that the conversation had taken a different turn.

'I most certainly do,' said Mr. Budd. 'More so now than ever before. Now get along, I've got a lot of work to do.'

The sergeant took his departure, and the big man settled himself more comfortably in his chair. For a man who had just stated that he was going to be busy, he certainly spent the next hour in a most extraordinary fashion; for with his chin sunk on his broad chest he lolled in his chair, to all intents and purposes oblivious to his surroundings. His brain was working rapidly, fitting together the information he had acquired and gradually achieving a coherent pattern.

A tap at the door roused him from his reverie. 'Come in,' he called, and a messenger entered.

'Nokes is downstairs, sir,' he announced. 'He wants to see you.'

' 'Nosy', eh?' murmured Mr. Budd, caressing his ample chin. 'I wonder what he wants. Shoot him up.'

The messenger departed, and the big man stared thoughtfully at his blotting pad. 'Nosy' Nokes existed precariously by occasionally bringing items of information to the police. He was an unpleasant little man, skinny and wizened, with watery eyes and a constant sniff as though he had a perpetual cold in the head. But his items of news were usually authentic, and although the police regarded him with contempt they listened to what he had to say, and mostly acted upon it.

Many were the people languishing in prison who owed their incarceration to the furtive-eyed Mr. Nokes, although his name had not appeared at their trial or in any of the various reports concerning their particular offence. He figured under the vague inscription 'Information received'.

He shuffled into the cheerless office and stood deferentially in front of Mr. Budd. The stout superintendent eyed him. 'Well, 'Nosy',' he grunted, 'what have you got hold of this time?'

'There's somethin' big 'appenin'!' the little man said nasally. 'You know the Wapping lot, Sellini's gang, the Borough Boys, the Whitechapel Whippets?' Mr. Nokes ran through a long list of noted race gangs. 'Well, they're all bein' canvassed by someone.'

Mr. Budd sat up quickly. 'How d'you mean, canvassed?' he asked.

'Someone's ropin' 'em in fer somethin' or other. There's a lot of excitement goin' about, whispers and whatnot. I don't know exactly what's in the wind, but there's somethin'. Sellini's disappeared.

Nobody knows where 'e is. Maybe he's at the bottom of it.'

Mr. Budd could have informed him where Tony Sellini was, but he refrained. 'Can't you tell me any more than that?'

The little man shook his head. 'No, I don't know no more. I may get a line on it, but I thought I'd better let you know straight away. There's somethin' brewin'. I'll try and find out what it is, but I'll 'ave to go careful. The 'boys' are a bit suspicious of me, and if they thought I was passin' on anythin' to the 'busies' me throat'd be slit. I gotta be careful. But you can take it from me there's somethin' in the wind. Deptford's 'ummin' like a bee-'ive, and so's Poplar and Nottin' Dale. You can feel it.'

'I'll warn Divisions,' said Mr. Budd. 'See if you can get any further information, 'Nosy', and let me know at once.'

'I'll do me best,' said the informer, 'but I've gotta go careful.'

'Go as careful as you like,' grunted Mr. Budd, 'but get hold of somethin' tangible.'

He dismissed the little man and sat for

some time after he had gone, pondering over his news. Was the cause of the excitement he had mentioned something connected with the Silver Horseshoe?

He got in touch with his own area and passed the information on, afterwards warning the other members of the 'big four'. A hasty conference was called between the four superintendents who each controlled one of the areas into which London was divided, at the expiration of which the news was transmitted to the divisional officer in charge of the various police stations in the districts affected.

'That's all we can do at the moment,' said Superintendent Halliday, a thin, weary-faced man. 'I wonder what's up?'

'A gang fight, probably,' grunted one of his fellow officials. 'These fellows break out every now and again and try and wipe each other off the map. Pity they don't succeed; it'd make our task a lot easier.'

'I expect you're right, Shaw,' agreed the third member of the 'big four'. 'Nokes may think it's something big, but these fellows couldn't think of anything big.

They haven't got the brains of a louse between 'em.'

'Somebody may be usin' 'em,' said Mr. Budd. 'Somebody who *has* got brains.'

'You've been reading books!' Superintendent Halliday accused. 'There's no such thing as the master criminal. You ought to know that!'

'Well, we shall see,' said Mr. Budd good-humouredly. 'I've got a hunch the Silver Horseshoe are plannin' a final coup, and this is part of it.'

His companions were sceptical, but by four o'clock on the following day they had changed their attitude, for by then the whole country was ringing with the colossal coup the Silver Horseshoe had successfully carried out.

* * *

Mr. Jacob Bellamy paced up and down the study of his small house, his shaggy brows drawn together, his huge hands clasped behind him. In the little lane at the back a patient man stood, watchful and alert, and in the front another supported himself against the lamp-post, equally alert and watchful.

The bookmaker knew they were there and the fact irritated him. Mr. Budd had placed them as guards, despite his protest.

'I've got a certain responsibility regardin' you,' he said in answer to old Jacob's argument. 'I'm not goin' to get reprimanded if anythin' happens to you. Those men'll remain where they are, and when they go two others'll take their place, and that's that!'

Mr. Bellamy had slammed down the receiver, annoyed to think that he was being treated like a child. He was still convinced that he was capable of looking after himself.

At nine o'clock Peter Ashton put in an appearance in answer to a peremptory invitation from the old man. 'Did you see 'em?' grunted Bellamy as he escorted his visitor into the study. 'One at the front and one at the back, as if I was royalty, or a blinkin' film star!'

'Budd's having Marjorie watched as well,' said Peter.

'Well, that's sensible!' retorted the bookmaker. 'She's a girl. But I'm capable of takin' care of meself. I remember the days when I've cracked a few policemen's skulls!'

Peter refrained from argument. He considered that Mr. Budd's precautions were wise. 'What have you sent for me for?' he inquired as the old man poured out drinks.

'I've been thinking' said Bellamy. 'You'll remember my idea was that we should fight these people ourselves? I'm carryin' on!'

'How?' Peter demanded.

'You 'eard what that feller Piggott said, the other night at your cottage — about Lord Sevenways bein' responsible for this racket?'

Peter nodded.

'Well, and you 'eard what that skinny sergeant said when he explained 'ow 'e'd followed those two fellers from Sevenways's place?'

'Yes, I heard all that,' said the reporter.

'Well, I sent for you because I wanted your permission to let me go down to the cottage and have a nose round.'

'You can have permission, with plea-sure, Jacob,' said Peter. 'But I don't think you ought to take the risk.'

'What d'you think I am, all of you — a lily?'

'No!' retorted Peter seriously. 'But I do think you ought to realise you're in danger. These people have had several goes at you, and if it hadn't been for Budd they'd have got you at Gatwick.'

'That doesn't say they're goin' to get another chance,' growled the old man. 'I'm not goin' to sit here and let that lump of fat treat me as if I was a kid!'

'So what are you going to do when you get to the cottage?'

'See if I can't discover something,' said Bellamy. 'If this Lord Sevenways, or whatever his name is, is behind this racket, I'll give 'im such a pastin' that he'll wish he'd never been born!'

'You'll be followed,' warned Peter. 'You won't be able to go anywhere without those fellows knowing it.'

'Pah! If I ain't capable of givin' a couple of ruddy busies the slip, my name ain't Jacob Bellamy!'

Peter shrugged. 'So far as I'm concerned,' he remarked, 'you can do as you like. But if you elude these two men you'll only run into two more. Leek and another fellow are already down at the cottage.'

'The whole of Scotland Yard can be there, so far as I'm interested!' snapped the bookmaker. 'I shan't interfere with Leek as long as he don't interfere with me. What about coming with me?'

'Can't be done!' Peter declared. 'I've got to go back to the office and write two columns before the deadline. I should be there now, as a matter of fact, but your message was so urgent.'

'All right, I'll go on me own!' said Bellamy. 'Maybe I'll supply you with a headline or two before the mornin'.'

'Let's hope it isn't an obituary notice!' retorted Peter.

'P'raps it will be, cock!' retorted the old man. 'Somebody's!'

Peter was concerned in his mind as he drove back to Fleet Street, but Bellamy was one of those people whom it was impossible to argue with. After all, it was doubtful whether he would succeed in shaking off the experienced watchers, and even if he did there was Leek and another police officer at the cottage.

He reached the offices of the *Morning Mail* and made his way to the reporters' room. Going over to a desk, he sat down to type his copy. It was twelve o'clock when he finished, and he was gathering up the sheets preparatory to taking them into the news editor when the drama critic put in an appearance.

'Hello, Stone!' said Peter. 'What was the show like?'

'Lousy!' grunted Mr. Joshua Stone.

'Who wrote it, Shakespeare?' asked Peter innocently, and Mr. Stone scowled.

'You know very well it wasn't Shakespeare. Shakespeare is the only dramatist whose plays are worth seeing.'

'Have you ever troubled to analyse one of his plots?' Peter smiled. 'They're sheer, unadulterated melodrama. If a modern author dared to use a plot like *Hamlet* or *Macbeth* you'd slate him down to the ground.'

'You know nothing about literature!'

305

said the drama critic loftily.

'How should I?' said Peter, grinning. 'I'm a crime reporter.'

'Then you ought to have gone to the play this evening,' snapped Mr. Stone. 'A greater crime has never been committed!' He took his departure to deliver his criticism which he had written in a taxi on the way down, and Peter rose to deliver his own copy.

At that moment the communicating door of the news room burst open and a shirt-sleeved 'sub' thrust in his head. 'Sorbet wants you, Ashton. Concerning the Cloudland Advertising Company. Message just come through: night watch-man at the aerodrome clubbed and six planes stolen — vanished into thin air, literally!'

'Bang goes a night's sleep!' Peter grumbled, and presented himself to Mr. Sorbet.

17

A Shock for Lord Sevenways

Broad Acres lay under a night sky still and silent, for it was past midnight and the household had retired to bed. But at least one member of the establishment was wakeful.

Lord Sevenways sat by the open window of his darkened room and stared into the warm night. The breach between himself and his wife, beginning on that night when he had witnessed her stealthy departure from the house to meet the unknown man in the grounds, had gradually widened. He was still polite, but with a touch of frigidness which had not been present before. Again and again he had caught sight of Sybilla regarding him with hurt surprise, but his pride had kept his lips sealed, and she had put his altered manner down to some worry which he had not confided to her. Never for an instant did she suspect that her rendez-vous had been witnessed.

Many times since, Sevenways had come to a decision to tax his wife and demand an explanation, but at the last moment his courage had failed him. Nicholas Melville, ninth Earl of Sevenways, was devoted to the young wife he had brought back from America and could imagine no joy in life without her.

But this could not go on. He would have to screw up his courage and demand an explanation.

She had gone to her room early, pleading a headache, and since dinner he had been left to his own devices, wondering whether tonight would see another clandestine meeting. He had become a spy in his own house!

If only he could bring himself to regard the matter sanely. He had planned so many times what he would do. In the morning, before she went downstairs, he would go into her room and face the thing with her. Even if she loved this other man, he could bear to know it, he told himself, if she did not conceal it from him.

He started. Something was moving in the darkness of the garden. He could see a faint shadow superimposed on the darker shadow of the trees and shrubbery. He rose to his feet, straining his eyes, his heart beating faster. A leaden weight settled at the pit of his stomach and his mouth became dry.

The figure moved across the lawn and Sevenways listened — listened for the sound of his wife's room door opening, her passage across the landing, the creak of a stair. But all was silent. There was no sound in the house except the faint pulsing of the big clock in the hall below.

Perhaps she had already gone, silently and stealthily, without his hearing her light steps on the thick carpet. He moved over to the door, hesitated, then with infinite care stepped out into the dark corridor.

He felt his way to the head of the stairs and paused, peering over to the dark well beneath. And then he made up his mind to go out and tackle this man, force him to tell the truth! He made his way down the staircase, crossed the hall, and noiselessly drew the massive door. The warm night air fanned his flushed face and he stepped out.

The scent of the spring flowers came to his nostrils as he moved round to the lawn across which he had seen the figure glide. That moving figure had been no trick of his imagination. Somewhere in the silence and the shadows lurked a man waiting for the second party to the appointment.

Sevenways moved into the shadow of a shrubbery, tiptoeing stealthily along, hating the whole wretched business. But he must find out! He must be certain!

The night was very still; not a leaf moved. The faint rustle of some nocturnal animal startled him and he paused. A clock somewhere in the distance faintly struck a single note. One!

He crept forward again, following the line of the shrubbery to the point where he had seen the figure emerge. But there was no sign of anyone. The garden was deserted and still. There before him was the tree under which he had witnessed the previous meeting. There was nobody standing there now. Could he have been mistaken?

He stopped, glancing about uncertainly. The man he had seen had crossed the lawn. Should he follow? It would bring him out of the shadows and in plain view of anyone lurking about.

He took a step forward, and then swung round as a rustle came from behind him. A dark figure loomed up and a large hand gripped him by the arm, while another was pressed suddenly over his mouth and nostrils, stifling the thin cry which rose to his throat.

'Keep still!' growled a voice. 'If you try to shout I'll break your ruddy neck!'

Sevenways struggled helplessly. The arms that held him were powerful and he was lifted like a child and carried through the shrubbery, his mind a conflicting whirl of surprise, indignation, and fear.

★ ★ ★

Next to Ascot, Goodwood is, perhaps, the most beautiful course in the country. It is miles from anywhere and boasts magnificent views over parts of Sussex and Hampshire. The saying 'Glorious Goodwood' is not a misnomer; and on this, the first of the four days' meeting, the sun was shining in a cloudless sky.

As usual the course was crowded. Tattersalls was a kaleidoscopic picture of gaily hued gowns and flimsy hats, enhanced by the conventional grey morning coat and topper. The surging murmur of voices, punctuated by the occasional cadence of a laugh, and less pleasantly by the raucous cries of the bookmakers, filled the air.

Everybody who was anybody, and a great number of people who were nobodies except in their own estimation, was present bent on a pleasurable day's racing under almost ideal conditions.

The horses had already paraded for the first race, a one-mile event, and had gone into the saddling enclosure. The crowd in twos and threes and larger groups was moving slowly from the paddocks to the stand. Bookmakers were shouting the odds in the cheaper enclosures, and the whole colourful and noisy proceedings associated with a racecourse were in full swing.

Desert Sand was the favourite — a four-year-old belonging to the popular owner, Sir Humphrey Wardly — and in spite of the odds of five to two, the betting was fast and furious, for the horse was considered a racing certainty.

'Where's Bellamy today?' remarked a professional backer to his companion as they passed the bookmaker's stand and saw that it was presided over by a stranger.

'I don't know,' answered his companion. 'Perhaps the shock of that business at Gatwick upset him. Are you backing the favourite in this race?'

'I'm not betting at all in this race,' he replied. 'I'm only having one bet today, in the Stewards' Cup. If it wins I shall have cleared a nice little bit.'

They made their way to the stands and took their places, and a few seconds later the bell rang. It was a perfect start, and the field kept an almost straight line until they came to the bend and turned into the straight. Here the powerful Desert Sand shot ahead, and maintaining his lead passed the post by three lengths ahead of his nearest rival. The win was greeted with a roar of delight that drowned the groans of the few who had not followed the money. The numbers went up, and for the next quarter of an hour the bookmakers were busy paying out.

'Popular start for the meeting,' said Swinton of the *Winning Post* as he left the press stand in search of refreshments.

'It was a certainty,' declared 'Captain Tattenham' of the *Wire*. 'Every paper tipped it. I made it my best of the day.'

They made their way to the refreshment tent, discussing the entries for the next race which, although they didn't know it then, was never destined to be run.

The majority of the people in the better class enclosures had had lunch and were strolling in the paddocks, smoking and chatting, when the low hum of the planes became audible. They appeared from the west, flying in rather scattered formation:

six of them, little specks in the cloudless sky at a high altitude. No one took very much notice of them. They passed over the course and the faint noise of the engines receded and died away.

At that moment the horses were brought out to parade for the second race, and any small amount of interest the planes might have caused was forgotten in the all-absorbing occupation of picking the likely winner.

In the cheaper enclosures, however, the advent of the planes had produced a certain tenseness among a number of rather flashily dressed men whom Mr. Budd would have recognised instantly as those referred to by 'Nosy' Noakes. They congregated into little groups and began to whisper excitedly, glancing furtively about them. It was noticeable that each was equipped with a hiker's haversack slung across their shoulders, an incongruous article that contrasted rather peculiarly with the shoddy smartness of their attire.

The horses were moving slowly down to the start when the planes came once more in sight. This time they were flying low and spread into an almost straight line. They came on, heading for the course, the roar of their engines drowning the raucous cries of the bookmakers and sending heads turning in startled surprise in the direction of the din.

One of the group of stewards frowned angrily. 'I shall certainly complain to the Air Ministry. Whoever's responsible, it's damn stupid. My God, look at that!' he said in stunned amazement.

The oncoming line of planes had reached the fringe of the crowd and suddenly, from the rear of each machine, shot billows of yellowish-green smoke. The mantle of vapour trailed out behind them; and as they advanced, roaring a hundred and fifty feet above the startled people below, they spread a canopy of thin, misty cloud that covered the stands, the course, the enclosures, everywhere, with a fog-like vapour.

It began to fall, gently and softly: a swirling, sinister yellow-green smoke enveloping the thousands of people present in an acrid cloud. And where it had passed they dropped, like flies.

In less than three minutes it was all over, that amazing and tremendous happening which was to startle the people of the world and fill the papers for days to come.

Like corn before a reaping machine, the vast crowd succumbed to the gas which was pouring in a poisonous cloud from the tails of the six machines. Some tried to run, screaming, but they were caught in the deadly vapour before they could cover more than a few yards. Bookmakers fell from their stands to lie motionless amid the punters who had been betting with them. In the stewards' room a frantic secretary tried desperately to telephone. The line was dead! Policemen, racecourse officials and press men were powerless.

The planes turned, came back, and landed one after the other on the course. The noise of the engines diminished and faded to silence; and when they were stilled a deathly hush hung over the whole place.

Goodwood was like a city of the dead.

In the paddocks and Tattersalls people lay just as they had dropped. The stands were covered with the scattered forms of unconscious humanity. At the starting tape horses and jockeys lay sprawling, and over all hung that iridescent miasma of yellowish-green vapour, a poisonous pall which the light breeze moved sluggishly.

It was a nightmare scene, unreal, rendered the more so by the figures which descended from the cockpit of each stationary plane. Rubber masks with great mica eyepieces covered their heads which, together with the snout-like tube running to the oxygen bag, gave them the appearance of weird animals. They carried sacks, and as they hurried up the course they were joined by fifty or sixty men with similar headgear. These came from the cheaper enclosures, and the gas masks provided a solution to the haver-sacks which they had carried on their backs.

From one of the planes more sacks were produced and handed round swiftly. A man who was apparently the leader of this gigantic enterprise spoke hurriedly, his voice muffled by the mask he wore.

'Be quick! Make a clean sweep. We've got roughly between fifteen and twenty minutes before the effects of the gas will begin to wear off. It'll wear off quicker because of this confounded breeze! Now jump to it!'

The men hurried away, and although there was bustle there was no confusion. Everything had been planned to the last detail. Each man had a section in which he worked rapidly, stripping the unconscious and recumbent figures in that area of every valuable they possessed and cramming them into the bag which he carried for the purpose.

The greatest robbery ever known had been successfully planned and carried out!

18

A Stupendous Coup!

The news came through to the *Morning Mail* at half past three, and was received by the entire occupants of that alert and industrious building in stunned surprise.

'Impossible!' said Peter Ashton. 'It couldn't have happened!'

'It *has* happened!' snapped Mr. Sorbet excitedly. 'What a sensation! The entire crowd at a race meeting put to sleep by gas and robbed! Think of it, man!' His voice rose shrilly. 'It's the greatest sensation of the year, of any year! These people must have got away with thousands, millions! Get down to Goodwood as fast as you can and get me a story.'

Peter's story duly appeared in company with dozens of others. Every newspaper in 'The Street' vied with each other in the matter of startling headlines. Provincial correspondents kept the telephone wires crackling, and excitement seethed through the country.

Mr. Sorbet had been right: a sensation it was! People discussed it in their homes, in buses, in tubes, at street corners, in public houses. Theatres and cinemas were empty. The newspapers were besieged with telephonic and personal inquiries for further news. The steward of the Jockey Club summoned a hasty meeting to discuss the unparalleled and unheard-of event.

In the immediate vicinity of Goodwood, doctors rushed to the private houses and hospitals to which the victims of the Silver Horseshoe's astounding coup had been taken. The majority of them were very little the worse for their experience. The gas used had been harmless. It had brought unconsciousness quickly, but they had recovered with no other ill effects than a violent headache and a feeling of sickness. Except, that was, for a few with very weak hearts who had succumbed and died.

Peter Ashton discovered that all telephone wires to the course had been cut just prior to the arrival of the planes.

It was the size and audacity of the robbery which caused the sensation.

Mr. Budd heard of it from an agitated and shocked chief constable as he was wearily leaving Scotland Yard to go home for a brief rest.

'It's terrible!' said the grey-haired official. 'Such a wholesale robbery has never been known!'

Mr. Budd was remembering 'Nosy' Noakes' information of the previous day. 'Well, we know part of the people responsible, anyhow ... ' The house telephone rang and he picked up the receiver.

It was the assistant commissioner, curt and a little caustic. 'Come to my office at once! You've heard of this latest outrage, of course?'

'Yes, sir,' said Mr. Budd. 'I've heard!' He hung up and made his way ponderously to Colonel Blair's room.

'Come in, Superintendent!' he said testily. 'This Goodwood business was organised by the Silver Horseshoe! In several instances a little silver replica of a horseshoe was found on the people who had been robbed. We've got to do something at once! There'll be a frenzied outcry against police methods in all the newspapers. You know that?'

'Yes, sir, I know that,' replied the big man wearily.

'Well, what are you going to do?' Colonel Blair snapped. 'You're in charge of the case!'

The big man pulled forward a chair and without asking permission sat down. 'Listen, sir,' he said, 'I *know* the persons responsible, and I can pull 'em in just whenever I like.'

Colonel Blair gaped at him. 'You know who is behind the Horseshoe?' he gasped.

'Yes, I know,' Mr. Budd said, nodding slowly. 'But I want to prevent a scandal. And if I move prematurely there's goin' to be one of the biggest scandals that ever happened!'

'Scandal? Who is it?' demanded the assistant commissioner.

The stout man leaned forward und began speaking rapidly, and as he proceeded Colonel Blair's face changed from uncertainty to incredulity, surprise, and eventually to open amazement. 'You're sure of this?' he demanded.

'Yes, I'm sure!' said the detective. 'But I'm not sure enough to make an arrest.'

'No, no! We must be careful, very careful indeed,' said the assistant commissioner, stroking his small moustache nervously. 'This is going to cause a bigger sensation than this infernal robbery at Goodwood!'

'That was inevitable,' said Mr. Budd. 'I wonder why it never happened before. Look at the opportunity and reward! A racecourse crowded with people carrying valuables and money worth millions and millions.'

'Well, it's been done now,' said Colonel Blair.

'Much easier than a 'smash and grab' raid,' said Mr. Budd. 'That's what science has done for 'em. Put weapons in the hands of criminals that they'd never have had before.'

The assistant commissioner made an impatient gesture. 'No doubt you're right to a certain extent,' he said irritably. 'But that doesn't get us anywhere. I appreciate that you've got to move circumspectly in this particular instance, but we've got to have something for the newspapers, a sop to show that we're doing things.'

'I'm gettin' on to the Flyin' Squad,' said Mr. Budd, 'and I'm havin' these little race gang crooks pulled in, the ones that Noakes mentioned. That'll be enough to keep the public quiet for a bit.'

Colonel Blair's face cleared. 'Deal with that at once then, Superintendent, and keep me posted concerning what you've just told me. Incredible!' He was still shaking his head unbelievingly when Mr. Budd took his leave and made his way back to his own office.

Mr. Budd got busy on the house telephone, and the immediate result of his energy was the appearance in certain districts of innocuous-looking trades-men's vans and decrepit cars which sped into narrow streets, stopped, and emerged again carrying sullen-eyed passengers.

By midnight the cells at Cannon Row were full of a collection of crooks of varying nationalities. In the small hours of the morning Mr. Budd went to survey the catch. They were brought up and paraded in the charge of guards. They were mostly members of race gangs and he eyed them sleepily.

'Now look here,' he said in his best official voice. 'You're in bad trouble! You're wanted for bein' concerned in a robbery at Goodwood racecourse this afternoon, at which some people died. When you're brought up before the magistrate he's goin' to take a serious view of it! So if you're wise you'll tell all you know. Who put you up to this?'

'We ain't squealing,' muttered a greasy-haired, sallow-faced man sullenly. 'You've got no proof we was mixed up in the Goodwood robbery.'

'You don't know what I've got!' snapped Mr. Budd. 'You were seen on the course and you weren't seen after. I've got enough evidence to put you all away for years. But the man who gives me some help'll probably get off with a light sentence. Now, what about it?'

There was a shuffling of feet, but nobody replied.

'Take 'em back to the cells,' Mr. Budd ordered. 'We'll see what they have to say in court tomorrow.'

The prisoners were led away, and the big man went back to his office in Scotland Yard. A report had come in to the effect that the six aeroplanes had been found abandoned in a field on the outskirts of Hampshire. A farmer had seen them come down and had gone to watch curiously. He had been attacked and clubbed to unconsciousness.

Mr. Budd frowned when he read the report. The planes had been stolen in the first place, hidden somewhere until they had been used at Goodwood, and abandoned afterwards and their valuable contents removed, probably by cars which had been waiting in the vicinity of the meadow in which they had come down.

There was a tap at the door and a messenger entered. 'The inspector in charge at Gannon Row would like to see you, sir,' said the man.

Mr. Budd stifled a weary yawn. 'All right, I'll come at once.'

In the charge room he found the

inspector waiting. 'One of those men we pulled in, sir,' said the man. 'He wants a word with you.'

'I thought somebody would squeal,' Mr. Budd smiled grimly, 'if we let 'em stew. Bring him up.'

The man came — a little, dark-eyed, wizened man. He looked round nervously. 'I couldn't say nothin' before the others,' he whispered in a low voice. 'I'd get a bashin' if they knew. But if you can get me off I'm willin' to tell all I know.'

'I can't promise anythin',' said Mr. Budd, 'but I'll see that whatever you say is used in your favour.'

'Well, listen. I can tell you where we're supposed to get our share.'

The superintendent became suddenly alert. 'Spill it!'

The squealer, whose name was Garcio, looked nervously about him and his voice dropped to a whisper. 'An office in Tilbury Street,' he said. 'Belongin' to a feller called J. Stanmore. We were to go there tomorrow night to get our share of this afternoon's business.'

'When?'

'Tomorrow night at twelve,' answered the unpleasant Garcio.

'How many of you were in this job?' demanded the big man.

'Sixty of us,' answered Garcio, and Mr. Budd whistled softly.

'But you weren't all goin', were you?'

'No,' Garcio answered. 'Only one feller from each gang. They was gettin' the whole boodle and dishin' it out to us after.' Garcio paused, his face working. 'You won't let on where you got the information, will you? The boys'd kill me if they thought I'd squeaked.'

The detective looked at him a little contemptuously. 'We don't give that sort of thing away here.'

'And you'll speak up for me? I wouldn't mind so much for meself, but I got a wife and three children — '

Mr. Budd cut short the ancient excuse with a gesture. 'I'll do what I can,' he promised, and Garcio was led back to his cell.

Weary but satisfied, Mr. Budd left Scotland Yard at dawn to seek his small villa at Streatham for a well-earned rest.

He slept dreamlessly, for he knew that the end was in sight, and that the morrow would bring about the destruction of the organisation that had been responsible for the death of John Arbinger.

* * *

Mr. Budd was up early. Big Ben was chiming nine when he turned in through the Whitehall entrance to Scotland Yard and made his way up to his office. A thin and lugubrious figure was perched on the hard visitor's chair when he entered.

'Hello!' growled Mr. Budd. 'Why have you left your post?'

'Bellamy!' answered the sergeant despondently. 'I thought I'd better come and tell you at once. That feller's pinched Sevenways — and I don't know what 'es done with 'im!'

Mr. Budd compressed his lips. 'Tell me all about it!' he snapped, moving ponderously to his chair.

'It's all a bit of a jumble,' Leek confessed. 'I was on duty the night afore last, keepin' an eye on Broad Acres, when

Bellamy turns up. He says that Peter Ashton 'ad given him permission to use his cottage. He said he'd already seen Sergeant Eaton and 'e wanted to give us a hand. Naturally I told 'im we didn't want no assistance. I didn't want no amateurs messin' things up, so I told 'im to make 'isself scarce.'

He paused for commendation, but Mr. Budd only grunted. 'Go on,' he said shortly.

'Well, he went away,' continued Leek. 'I'd gone off to get a bit of a rest and Eaton had taken me place, but there was no sign of Bellamy at the cottage. I thought like as not he'd taken the 'int. I 'ad a sleep and went back to relieve Eaton, but couldn't find 'im nowhere. Then suddenly I saw poor Eaton stumblin' towards me. 'is nose was bleedin' and 'e 'ad a black eye. Eaton told 'e'd been watching, and seen Lord Sevenways acting suspicious like, sort of prowling about the grounds of Broad Acres. He'd been watching him when there was a bit of a rumpus and a huge man sprang out of the shrubbery and attacked his lordship. Eaton couldn't make up his mind at first whether to interfere or not, but 'e saw this big feller — Bellamy — pick up 'is lordship and carry 'im off like a kid. So 'e tried to interfere, but Bellamy pasted 'im good and proper. And now Bellamy's gone and so 'as Sevenways.'

'Why didn't you report this before?' demanded Mr. Budd irritably.

'Well, I was 'opin',' explained Leek, 'to find out somethin'. Lady Sevenways telephoned the police, and they've been searchin' the country in the vicinity of the 'ouse. There's a rare to-do, I can tell you.'

'Haven't I got enough to attend to without these amateurs puttin' their oar in and spoilin' everythin'?' Mr. Budd groaned. 'What in the world did Bellamy want to interfere for?'

'It's my opinion that 'e's got it into 'is 'ead that Lord Sevenways is behind the 'orseshoe business,' said Leek. 'You remember what that feller Piggott said the night they nearly popped us off?'

'I remember what everybody said!'

snapped Mr. Budd. 'Be quiet for a minute!'

He sat hunched up behind his desk lost in thought. After a few minutes he roused himself, picked up his telephone and asked to be put through to Peter Ashton at the *Morning Mail* offices.

The reporter listened in amazement to his news. 'I'd no idea the old man was contemplating anything so drastic!' he exclaimed. 'When I let him use my cottage I thought he was only going to nose about, and wouldn't do any harm.'

'There's no knowin' what harm he's done!' said Mr. Budd. 'And I'd got all my plans nicely fixed up. This is goin' to lead to trouble, Mr. Ashton. Can you think of anywhere where he might have taken him?'

'Not really. Have you tried Bellamy's house?'

'No. But I'll try now.'

'I'll be along in a minute,' said Peter. 'I want to see you, anyway.'

'Don't you go botherin' me today!' snarled Mr. Budd. 'I'm not in the mood for reporters!' He banged down the receiver.

Picking it up again, he tried Jacob Bellamy's private number, but there was no reply. A call to his office resulted in the information that he had not been there for two days. The stout detective leaned back in his chair and lighted a cigar. Under the soothing influence of the rank tobacco he regained something of his equanimity.

'You get back to Broad Acres, Leek, and report to me at once if anything's discovered concernin' Bellamy's whereabouts or Sevenways's.'

Leek had been gone about five minutes when Peter Ashton arrived. He looked tired and weary, having had little rest since the news of the Goodwood raid had broken.

'If I'd known Bellamy was going to do a crazy thing like that I'd have stopped him!' he declared.

'Never mind him for the moment,' said Mr. Budd. 'D'you want to be in at the end of the Horseshoe?'

'Of course I do!' he answered quickly.

'D'you mean you're near the end?'

'Yes, Mr. Ashton, I'm very near the end. I'm going to take the second-in-command of the Silver Horseshoe tonight.'

The tired lines vanished from Peter Ashton's face.

'At twelve o'clock I shall find him in a little office in Tilbury Street,' Mr. Budd told him. 'If you'd like to be here soon after eleven you can come with me.'

'You bet I'll be here!' said Peter. 'What about the big noise — do you know him, too?'

'Yes, I know the king pippin,' said Mr. Budd. 'But I don't think the big noise is going to be there. I'm goin' to have difficulty about that.'

'D'you mean you don't know where to find him?'

'No, that's not my difficulty,' murmured Mr. Budd. 'My difficulty is to prevent a scandal!'

Peter tried hard to get him to explain, but he would say no more.

'You'll know everythin' in due course,' he remarked. 'And don't go tryin' to do anythin' on your own,' he warned. 'I'm not standin' for any more amateur interference. I've had enough of it in this case.'

Peter absorbed the stricture without protest. Then a thought struck him.

'So you won't be using Sellini, after all?'

'No, I don't think we'll need to,' Mr. Budd answered. 'Which is tough on Sellini, because it means he'll stay put in Cannon Row until he's transferred to Pentonville for a longer sojourn.'

He sat for some time after Peter had gone, and then, rousing himself, he became very busy indeed. From a drawer in his desk he took a large folder, labelled in his sprawling writing 'Silver Horseshoe Notes'. It was full of typewritten reports, cablegrams, and scraps of paper covered with Mr. Budd's almost illegible writing. For a long time he sat, carefully reading through various items and jotting down notes on a pad beside him. Presently he closed the folder and put it away again, and then he set to work to make arrangements for the raid.

The evening brought drizzling rain that looked as if it was likely to continue all night. It had been necessary to request the co-operation of the city police, for Tilbury Street lay outside the area under the control of Scotland Yard. Mr. Budd had a long interview with a superintendent from the Old Jewry Headquarters. He was taking six of his own men, and the city force was providing an equal number.

'Twelve men should be sufficient,' he said. 'With me it's thirteen.'

'You're evidently not superstitious,' commented Peter Ashton, when he arrived soon after eleven and heard this.

'Well, it's goin' to be unlucky for someone,' said Mr. Budd. 'Come on, it's time we was goin'.'

They went down to where the police car was waiting, the raiding party already in their seats. The driver had his instructions, and they set off.

It was twenty minutes past eleven when they reached the city headquarters in Old Jewry, and here Mr. Budd held a brief consultation with the inspector in charge of the city men.

'We'll leave the cars a hundred yards away in Service Lane,' he said, 'and cover the rest of the distance on foot. I want a man posted at each end of Tilbury Street and four at the back of the buildin' in which Stanmore's got his office. I've been studyin' an ordnance map, and although there doesn't seem to be any way out that way, I'm not takin' any chances.'

The rain was falling more heavily, and there was not a living thing in sight as the little band of men halted at the corner of the street and peered down the narrow, deserted length.

'Stop everybody from leavin',' ordered Mr. Budd to the two men who were to guard either end. 'Nobody's to pass you, you understand?' The detectives nodded, and hurried to take up their positions.

'Come on, Mr. Ashton,' Mr. Budd said. 'We'll go over to that doorway and keep an eye on the front of the buildin'. As soon as anyone goes in I'll blow me whistle and the rest of you can follow me up the stairs. The office we want is at the top, and the name's Stanmore. I don't suppose there's anyone else in the buildin', so if you pinch all the people on the premises you won't go far wrong.'

They took up their positions at the place Mr. Budd had indicated, and a second later the street was empty once more, to all intents and purposes.

Peter glanced at his watch: twenty minutes to twelve. 'How did you get on to this fellow Stanmore?' he whispered, his lips close to Mr. Budd's ear.

In a voice which was scarcely audible Mr. Budd told him.

'But won't he know these fellows have been pinched?' asked the reporter. 'It's sure to have got around.'

'That doesn't signify,' answered Mr. Budd. 'He'll be there all right. He had to use those crooks, but he doesn't care what happens to 'em. In fact he'll be glad; there'll be less to share out. But he's got his own men, remember that. Those six aeroplanes had to be manned, and they weren't piloted by any of the fellers I've got in Cannon Row.'

His hand suddenly closed warningly on

Peter's arm and he breathed a word of caution. Following the direction of his eyes, Peter saw that a figure in a dark overcoat whose hat was pulled down was moving furtively along on the opposite pavement, shooting little darting glances about him. At the door of the building which housed the offices of Mr. Stanmore he paused for a moment, and the watchers thought he was about to enter; but he moved on again, disappearing into the shadowy darkness of the upper end of the street.

'That feller's like a Jack-in-the-box,' murmured Mr. Budd.

'Who was it?' whispered Peter.

'Didn't you recognise him? I did. I caught a glimpse of his face as he passed under that lamp — *Piggott!*'

'Didn't you expect to see him?' Peter inquired.

'No, Mr. Ashton, I did not,' answered Mr. Budd. 'Yet I suppose I ought. He's always turnin' up at odd places. He's the one thing about this business that I don't understand.'

He relapsed into silence and the

minutes passed slowly. A city clock struck twelve . . .

The sound of the bell had barely faded to silence before they heard a quick step. It came hurriedly from the upper end of the street and presently a man appeared, walking rapidly towards them. At the main door they were watching he stopped, gave a peculiar, almost inaudible rap with his knuckles, and vanished.

'That's one of 'em,' said Mr. Budd with satisfaction, 'and they've got a feller on the inside of that door waitin' to admit 'em as they come. That's worth knowin'.'

His podgy hand dived into the pocket of his overcoat and he assured himself that the pistol which he had secured from the firearms department that evening was there.

'How long are you going to wait?' whispered Peter.

'Some little time yet. We may as well bag the lot while we're about it.'

There was a short interval and then another man arrived, followed by a third and a fourth. Two more came at the expiration of a further five minutes, and when these last had been admitted Mr. Budd braced himself.

'Now!' he said, and stepping out from his place of concealment whistled softly.

Instantly he was joined by six other men who had been lurking in various doorways up the street. Approaching the door through which Mr. Stanmore's visitors had entered, Mr. Budd raised his hand and gave the same peculiar rap that each of the others had done. The door opened silently.

'Who's that?' whispered a voice from the darkness within, and without answering the stout detective grabbed the custodian and clapped a hand over his mouth, jerked him out into the street and thrust him into the arms of a waiting detective.

The surprised and terrified man opened his mouth to give the alarm, but his captor had deftly thrust a rolled-up handkerchief between his teeth. There was a faint jingle and a click and the prisoner's clawing hands were handcuffed behind him.

'Gag him and leave him here!' ordered

Mr. Budd in a low voice. 'And then follow me.'

With Peter at his side, he passed in to the pitch darkness of the passageway and stopped to listen. Silence. A faint ray of light pierced the gloom from a torch in the superintendent's hand, the lens of which had been covered with tissue paper except for one tiny pinpoint. Vaguely it illumined the beginning of a staircase.

'Go quietly,' murmured Mr. Budd to the men with him. 'We want to take 'em by surprise if possible.'

He began to mount, slowly and cautiously. The stairs creaked a little under his weight, but apparently the noise was not sufficient to give warning of their presence. They reached a landing and the big man played his torch on the doors.

'Further up,' he whispered, and they continued up a second flight.

Another landing was passed without discovering the suite occupied by Mr. Stanmore; and then, as they were climbing the last flight, catastrophe overtook them. One of the men stumbled, tried to recover his balance, and slipped noisily down three stairs.

A door above them was jerked open and a stream of light shot across the landing they were approaching. 'Is that you, Mayne?' said a voice. 'Why the hell can't you be more careful?'

A man appeared at the top of the narrow staircase, caught sight of the group, and uttered a startled exclamation. 'Look out!' he shouted. 'The 'busies' are here!'

There was a rush of feet, accompanied by a babble of voices, and the light above went out. A shot reverberated in the confined space and Mr. Budd's torch went flying from his hand. Two more shots followed in quick succession and Peter heard the bullets whine past his head and thud into the wall behind him.

'Come on!' said Mr. Budd, and led a rush up the remainder of the stairs.

19

The Brains of the Horseshoe

Peter never forgot that struggle in the darkness. It was impossible to see friend or foe. The stumbling of feet, the heavy breathing of men, the muttering of oaths and the thud of blows came from around him. Somebody bumped violently into him and almost knocked him off his feet. He staggered, recovered his balance, and came thudding up against a wall. A flash of flame and a report that deafened him came out of the darkness a foot in front of his face.

He opened his coat and searched an inner pocket for his torch. It was risky, but light was essential. Pandemonium was going on around him. The cracks of automatics mingled with cries of pain and muttered curses.

Peter pressed the button of his torch and sent a stream of light on the struggling figures that filled the landing. As he did so there was a crash and he saw two men who were fighting desperately overbalance and go bumping and slithering down the stairs. He made out the figure of Mr. Budd, his automatic clubbed, hitting out right and left; and then the torch was knocked from his hand and once more darkness enveloped the scene.

Somebody gripped his arm and kicked out at him, inflicting an agonising blow on the shin. He lashed out with his right and heard a grunt as his bunched fist landed on flesh. An arm was flung round his neck from behind and he fell heavily, with fingers digging into the flesh of his throat. His unknown assailant rolled over on top of him and Peter tried desperately to throw him off. The attempt was unsuccessful and he adopted another method. Letting himself go limp, he suddenly shot up his knees with all his force. The grip on his throat relaxed as his opponent shot over his head and landed with a heavy thud.

Peter staggered to his feet. It was

impossible to go on fighting in the dark, unable to tell friend from foe. The brief glimpse he had had of the landing before the torch had been struck from his fingers had shown him a door to his right. He felt his way to this, found it, and turning the handle, pushed it open. Passing his hand up and down the wall inside, he presently discovered the light switch and pressed it.

The single, rather dingy globe sprang to life and the light from the room spread fan-like over the landing.

Two of the raiding party were lying on the bare boards, groaning. In one corner crouched an unpleasant-faced man, spluttering blasphemy and nursing a leg from which blood was streaming. A detective was struggling with a burly man, and even as Peter looked he brought his truncheon down on his opponent's head and put an end to the fight. A furious uproar still sounded on the staircase. Mr. Budd had lost his hat, and his overcoat was half-torn from his back. He came panting towards the reporter.

'I think we're gettin' the better of 'em,' he panted.

An outburst of firing greeted his words and the plaster fell in a shower from the wall near at hand. The man who called himself Stanmore, his face streaked with blood, appeared from the midst of the mass of humanity on the staircase. He held an automatic pistol and he faced the big man and Peter, his mouth twisted into a malignant grin.

'You can take yours!' he snarled, and the muzzle of the weapon jerked up menacingly.

Two shots, following so swiftly on each other that they sounded as one, thundered from the lower landing, and Stanmore gave a convulsive start and staggered. The pistol in his hand exploded and the bullet passed Peter's cheek so close that he felt the wind of it.

A third shot came from the same direction as the other two, and Stanmore uttered a cry and spun round. He swayed unsteadily for a moment or two, his pistol falling with a clatter to the floor. And then his knees seemed to crumple and he fell forward, his clawing hands digging at the bare boards as his body twitched convulsively.

'I guess that's the third time I've saved your lives,' said a nasal voice, and they looked into the upturned face of Mr. Samuel K. Piggott.

'I'll talk to you in a minute,' Mr. Budd grunted, and moved to the head of the staircase.

The battle that had been raging there, and from behind which Mr. Piggott had fired, was practically over. A breathless and dishevelled sergeant detached himself from the melee and panted up to his superior.

'We've got 'em under, sir,' he reported jerkily. 'Is that the lot?'

'Yes, I think so,' murmured the big man, peering down. 'With this feller there should be seven.

'That's right, sir,' called one of the city men, wiping the blood from his face as he spoke. 'We've got six here.' He indicated the battered and sullen-faced men who stood helpless in the grasp of his companions.

'Take 'em down to the police car,' ordered Mr. Budd, straightening his coat.

'You stop here with me, Atkins.'

The sergeant nodded, and the superintendent looked round for his hat. It was lying over in an angle of the landing and Peter picked it up.

'Who's this fellow?' he asked, jerking his head towards Stanmore. 'Is he the brains of the outfit?'

'No, he isn't.' Mr. Budd took his badly treated headgear and jammed it on his head.

The American had joined them and was looking curiously at the man he had killed. He glanced at Mr. Budd. 'D'you know who he was?'

'Yes, I think I do. 'Kid' Leeming, wasn't he?'

'I didn't know you knew that,' Mr. Piggott murmured.

'There's quite a lot of things I know that you don't know!' retorted Mr. Budd. 'Now let's have a look round.'

He entered the dingy outer office, accompanied by the American, Peter and the sergeant. Glancing round the empty room, he sniffed disparagingly.

'Pretty dingy, but I suppose it suited his

purpose. A sort of clearing house. He only received his instructions and passed them on to the various members of the outfit.'

He went over to a door and tried the handle. It was locked.

'Maybe he's got the key on him,' he said. 'Have a look, Sergeant, will you?'

Sergeant Atkins went back to the body of the dead Stanmore, knelt down and searched him. Presently he returned with two linked keys.

'One of these'll be what you want, sir,' he said, handing them to Mr. Budd.

The big man selected the smaller key and thrust it into the keyhole. As he did so, Peter heard a movement from within. 'Look out! There's somebody in that room!'

A curious expression flitted across the face of the American as he, too, heard the movement.

Mr. Budd paused in the act of fitting the key to the lock. 'You'd better stand back,' he said. 'Whoever's behind here may be dangerous.'

As he spoke there came a creak from

within the room, followed by a sliding noise — the unmistakable sound of a window sash being raised.

'He's trying to escape by the window,' said Peter, and without waiting any longer Mr. Budd turned the key and threw open the door.

The shabby office was empty, but the window was wide open, and a dim figure showed for an instant as it swung across the sill.

'Come back!' cried Mr. Budd, and Peter sniffed the air, an incredible suspicion flashing to his brain. 'Come back!' cried the big man again. 'It's a thirty-foot drop. You'll — '

The figure at the window laughed and swung sideways. They saw it disappear; and then, as they rushed to the open casement, they saw a dark form clinging to a narrow iron ladder that was fastened to the wall.

'The fire escape!' exclaimed Peter, and even as he spoke the dark form faltered on its rapid downward journey. It swayed outward; there was a shrill scream that stirred the hair on the reporter's neck, and then a dark mass went hurtling to the stone paved yard thirty feet below. They heard it strike with a thud, and almost immediately afterward excited voices broke the silence and a light flashed out.

'Come on,' said Mr. Budd as he withdrew his head, and Peter saw that his big face was unusually pale. The detective raced across the inner office and across the outer room, and went stumbling down the staircase.

'Look out, sir,' said Sergeant Atkins. 'It's pitch dark. You'll break your neck if you aren't careful.'

'I've got a torch,' said Mr. Piggott, and a white ray focused on the hurrying form of Mr. Budd.

They reached the street level and paused. 'Which is the quickest way round?' panted the stout man.

'There's an alley a few yards further on,' answered the American. 'Follow me.'

He led the way, dived into a narrow passage, and presently came out into a short cul-de-sac. A brick wall ran across the end, in which was set a narrow door.

As they reached this barrier the door was opened.

'Who's that?' said a voice sharply.

'Superintendent Budd. Open up.'

The detective apologised and stood aside as they passed through the narrow aperture. He pushed past the man and hurried along the narrow concrete paved alley which ran along the back of the Tilbury Street buildings until he came to a group of three men who were staring down at a sprawling heap that lay at their feet. A widening pool of blood was slowly oozing over the hard surface.

'Dead?' asked the stout man, as he came breathlessly up.

'I'm afraid so, sir,' answered one of the men. 'Nobody could live after a fall like that.'

Mr. Budd bent forward, obscuring Peter's vision. The reporter heard the sharp intake of his breath. For a second or two he remained motionless, and then slowly he straightened up and turned.

'You want to know who was the brains behind the Silver Horseshoe, Mr. Ashton?' he asked soberly. 'Take a look!'

Peter stepped forward, guessing what he would see, and looked into the white face of Lady Sevenways!

★   ★   ★

Peter Ashton's dingy car sped swiftly up Putney Hill, swung through a wide gate, and came to a stop in front of the door of Marjorie Arbinger's house. The reporter got out and turned to the man who had accompanied him. 'We're the first to arrive, Jacob,' he said.

Mr. Bellamy grunted. 'Well, you was in such a darned hurry, cock,' he growled. 'I told you we'd be early.'

Peter walked up to the front door and rang the bell.

Three days had elapsed since the tragedy at Tilbury Street, and although the *Morning Mail* had come out with an exclusive story of the raid, at Mr. Budd's urgent request nothing had been printed concerning Lady Sevenways. Neither had any other newspaper mentioned her in connection with the Silver Horseshoe.

'Concentrate on Kid Leeming,' said the

big man, when Peter demanded information. 'He's your story. I'll tell you the one that's not for publication when I've got this business settled.'

The reporter heard no more until he received a telephone message asking him to be at Marjorie Arbinger's that morning.

He had been having breakfast when, to his surprise, a subdued and rather chastened Jacob Bellamy arrived at his little flat. His exploits at Broad Acres had nearly got him into serious trouble. He was reluctant to talk about it, but when Peter pressed him, he rather sheepishly explained.

'From what Piggott said, I thought this feller Sevenways was at the bottom of the business, cock. I thought I'd frighten him into tellin'. I took him to a friend of mine who keeps a sports club down at the Elephant and Castle and tried a little third-degree stuff. But I soon found he didn't know nothin'. The police discovered what I'd done with him, and you never 'eard such a fuss! Anybody'd think I was a criminal, the way I was treated!'

'Well, you can't go about abducting people,' said Peter reasonably.

'I was only tryin' to 'elp,' Jacob grumbled. 'It was just bad luck that I was wrong. It seems that Budd's got the whole thing straightened out.'

'He says he has,' answered the reporter. 'We shall know all about it when we see him this morning.'

When they were ushered into the long drawing room they found that in spite of being early they were not the first to arrive. Mr. Piggott was installed in a comfortable armchair, talking to Marjorie Arbinger.

'Good morning, Mr. Ashton,' said the American. 'How d'you do, Mr. Bellamy. So it's all over, eh? Well, I can't say I'm sorry.'

Peter looked at him curiously, wondering how this genial-faced man was mixed up in the matter. Mr. Piggott seemed to read his thoughts, for his smile broadened.

'You're curious about me, aren't you?' he chuckled. 'You won't have very long to wait before your curiosity is satisfied.'

357

'Is it true,' said Marjorie, 'that Lady Sevenways was the Silver Horseshoe?

'So Budd says,' answered Peter. 'I know very little about it. I suppose he's coming here this morning to tell us.'

The stout detective was announced at that moment and came in, followed by the melancholy Leek. He still looked tired and a little careworn. 'Mornin', everybody,' he said in his slow, ponderous drawl. 'I'm glad to see you're all punctual.' He smiled at the girl. 'I thought, Miss Arbinger,' he went on, 'that I'd have this little meetin' here so that you could hear all about it. Naturally as it concerns you so closely, you'd be curious.'

'It was very thoughtful of you,' she said.

Mr. Budd looked round, selected the largest chair, and settled himself comfortably. 'So you're goin' back to America on Friday,' he remarked, turning his head towards Mr. Piggott.

'How did you know that?' inquired the American.

'When a man books his passage on the *Brittanica* I naturally deduce that he's goin' to travel on the boat,' said the big man. 'And I won't insult your intelligence by tellin' you how I know that.'

'I thought I'd shaken off your watchers,' said Mr. Piggott genially.

'Well, you hadn't!' retorted Mr. Budd. He rubbed his chin and looked from one to the other. 'I suppose,' he continued, 'I'd better get on with it. Well, it's not a very long story, and some of it you know. It starts way back in America when Lord Sevenways fell in love and married the beautiful Sybilla Horton of the Ziegfeld Follies. That's the beginnin'. Some people thought she'd married him for his title, but they was wrong. She married him because she loved him. He had no money and his estate was mortgaged up to the hilt. It was as much as he could do to scrape together sufficient to live on. His father had been a heavy gambler on the racecourse, and when he died he left very little but debts. There was a horse runnin' in the Lincolnshire Handicap which everybody thought was a certainty, and to try and make enough to settle all his creditors, Sevenways raised every penny he could lay his hands on by borrowing and sellin' shares, and backed this horse to bring him in forty thousand pounds. Irish Fancy it was, and if you remember it was unplaced. That was the beginnin' of the Silver Horseshoe!

'Sybilla Horton had been brought up in Chicago. She was the daughter of old Dan Leeming, the Booze King, and human life to her was cheap. She'd seen men shot down daily until it meant nothin', and she knew the money that was to be made in the 'pay and live' racket. Her one ambition was to retrieve the fortunes of the Sevenways, clear off the mortgage on Broad Acres, and save her husband from having to sell his horses. She could see how worried he was, and bein' fond of him it worried her, too. She was wonderin' how she could help, when she had a letter from her brother sayin' he was in England and could he see her.

'Now her brother was a feller called Kid Leeming. He'd run several rackets in America and made the place pretty hot for him. His last exploit was in a 'snatch' game. They got hold of the baby daughter of a millionaire in Philadelphia, and held her to ransom. They got the money, but Leeming had to cut and run. He managed to get to England by devious routes and communicate with his sister. She asked him to meet her in the grounds of Broad Acres, and at that meeting the idea which developed into the Silver Horseshoe was born.

'It was her idea, but she couldn't run it without Leeming. He knew the ropes. She supplied the brains and he carried out her instructions. He took the office in Tilbury Street in the name of Stanmore and from there he controlled the organisation. Mostly she telephoned and he reported by telephone. Occasionally, when there was anythin' special on hand, they met at Broad Acres.

'You've got to remember, if you think it's queer that a woman should lend herself to a racket like this, that Lady Sevenways had spent her childhood among men like Leeming. Her father, old Dan, accordin' to the American police, was responsible for puttin' more men 'on the spot' than any other of the big shots.

To her curious mentality the end justified the means, and she didn't care who suffered so long as Sevenways and the estate was saved.

'How she started the racket, you know. She began with your father, Miss Arbinger. Curiously enough, he was the one man who had arranged to get her husband out of his trouble, and she didn't know this until after. When she did, she tried to make what reparation she could by sending you five thousand pounds through a shyster solicitor called Mervyn Holt.'

'So that's where it came from,' murmured the girl.

'Yes, that's where it came from. She also sent her own husband ten thousand, because that was her difficulty. She didn't know how to account to him for the money, so she sent it anonymously. At the back of her mind she had a plan. She invented a relation who was supposed to be very rich, and I believe it was her intention, when she'd collected as much as she wanted, to pretend that this feller had died and left her his fortune. That was the secret behind the Silver Horse-shoe. Just a woman's love for her husband that came out in a queer way.'

'Does Sevenways know this?' asked Peter.

'No, Mr. Ashton.' Mr. Budd shook his head. 'All he knows is that his wife's brother was behind the Silver Horseshoe. He didn't even know she had a brother. She kept that from him, havin' sufficient sense to realise that he wouldn't like havin' a gangster in the family. He thinks she was killed by accident, and it's broken him up. I've had a word with the commissioner and we're goin' to keep her name out of it for his sake. She's dead and nothin' can be gained by makin' a sensation. The whole thing has been explained to the home secretary and he's in agreement.

'I haven't got very much more to tell you. When Kid Leeming was runnin' his rackets in Chicago he came up against a feller who was at the head of a rival gang. They was both in booze at that time; it was before prohibition was lifted. This feller's name was Benion. He had a daughter, a very pretty girl, who all the fellers were after, and she fell for the Kid. He didn't treat her like a gentleman, and she was picked out of the water one night. She'd drowned herself because he'd left her and gone off with another girl. That's right, isn't it?' He turned sleepily towards Mr. Piggott.

'I guess that's right,' said the American soberly. 'Though how you found out beats me.'

'I've been interested in you for a long time,' said Mr. Budd, almost apologetically. 'One of my men took a photograph on my instructions and we forwarded copies to the American Detective Bureau. It wasn't difficult.'

'I see,' said the man who called himself Piggott. 'Yes, I'm Benion. I swore I'd get Kid Leeming, and I did! I traced him, and for weeks I've been waitin' for my opportunity.' He paused, and then, in a different tone: 'Well, I shall be glad to get back to America.'

'You're lucky to be able to go,' said Mr. Budd. 'I could hold you if I wanted to, but I'm not goin' to. We all owe you somethin'. You saved my life three times, for which I'm grateful. And from all accounts you weren't so bad as some of the others. You just went into the booze racket from a business point of view.'

Marjorie, who had been sitting silent, looked up suddenly. 'Lady Sevenways was rather a wonderful woman,' she said.

'Yes, she was,' agreed Mr. Budd. 'In her way and accordin' to her lights, she was a wonderful woman, as you say, Miss Arbinger.'

'What will happen to Sevenways?' asked Peter. 'I suppose he's taken it badly.'

'Very badly,' said the big man. 'He's in hospital at the moment, sufferin' from shock. When he recovers I expect he'll go abroad.' He sighed. 'Well, it's been a tryin' time,' he continued, 'but it's all over now. They're givin' me three weeks' holiday, and I can do with it.'

Mr. Piggott glanced at his watch and rose to his feet. 'If you'll excuse me, I'll be getting back to my hotel. I've a lot to do before I leave, so I don't suppose I shall see you again.'

'You won't find anybody trailin' you now,' said Mr. Budd, and the American's eyes twinkled.

'I will say,' he declared, 'that your policemen are wonderful! Goodbye, Miss Arbinger.' He looked slyly from the girl to Peter. 'If you'll let me know when the wedding takes place I'll mail a substantial present.'

Peter flushed. 'I don't know what you're talking about.'

'If you don't,' retorted Mr. Piggott, 'then you haven't got as much sense as I thought you had.' He walked over to the door. 'Goodbye, and good luck!' he said as he went out. And that was the last they ever saw of him.

'I must be goin', too,' remarked Mr. Budd, hoisting himself with difficulty out of his chair. 'Come on, Leek. Are you comin', Mr. Bellamy?' He looked at the huge figure of the bookmaker and his left eyelid drooped slyly.

'Yes, I must get along and attend to my business, cock,' he said. 'I've been neglecting it lately. So long, boy!' He waved a large hand at Peter. 'Goodbye for the present, Miss Arbinger.' He followed the stout man and the lean sergeant into the hall, and for some time after they were left alone neither Peter nor the girl spoke.

It was the reporter who broke the silence. 'If Piggott is leaving on Friday he'll reach New York on the following Wednesday,' he said.

'Yes, I suppose he will.' She looked at him in surprise.

'So if I sent him a cable next weekend,' continued Peter rapidly, 'it'll reach him soon after he lands. D'you think if I said August 10th it'd be too soon?'

'No, I don't think so,' she answered, and then she laughed. 'If that's a proposal it must be the queerest that's ever happened,' she said.

Peter walked firmly to the door, opened it, took the key from the outside, and turned it.

'Now,' he said, as his arms went round her, 'we can be more conventional.'

THE END

Books by Gerald Verner
in the Linford Mystery Library:

We do hope that you have enjoyed reading this large print book.

Did you know that all of our titles are available for purchase?

We publish a wide range of high quality large print books including:
Romances, Mysteries, Classics
General Fiction
Non Fiction and Westerns

Special interest titles available in large print are:
The Little Oxford Dictionary
Music Book, Song Book
Hymn Book, Service Book

Also available from us courtesy of Oxford University Press:
Young Readers' Dictionary
(large print edition)
Young Readers' Thesaurus
(large print edition)

For further information or a free brochure, please contact us at:
Ulverscroft Large Print Books Ltd.,
The Green, Bradgate Road, Anstey,
Leicester, LE7 7FU, England.
Tel: (00 44) **0116 236 4325**
Fax: (00 44) **0116 234 0205**

MISTER BIG

Gerald Verner

Behind all the large-scale crimes of recent years, the police believe there is an organising genius. The name by which this mysterious personality has become familiar to the press, the police and the underworld is Mister Big. When murder and kidnapping are added to his crimes, Superintendent Budd of Scotland Yard becomes actively involved. Eventually the master detective uncovers a witness who has actually observed and recognised Mister Big leaving the scene of a murder — but before he can tell Budd whom he has seen, he is himself murdered!

FIVE GREEN MEN

V. J. Banis

Nancy's vacation at her aunt's San Francisco mansion takes a nightmarish turn when she is attacked by a mysterious thief of ancient jade figurines. Her assailant's vows to kill her are very nearly successful more than once. Can she trust the stranger who has been following her ever since her arrival in the city, even though his intervention saves her life? Then she must contend with a murder she is powerless to stop, and the return of her father, who she'd been told had died when she was a child . . .

THE SCENT OF HEATHER

V. J. BANIS

Maggie and her sister Rebecca come to Heather House to recover from the drowning deaths of their two husbands. But the house seems to be haunted by the ghost of its one-time owner, Heather Lambert, the scent of the eponymous herb occasionally drifting through the air. As Maggie falls under the spell of the house, events take a more sinister turn when she narrowly survives an attempt on her life, and then the housekeeper is found murdered ... Can Maggie discover the secret of Heather House before it's too late?

HANGOVER HILL

Mary Wickizer Burgess

A young woman goes missing while taking a summer job in an old mining town in California's scenic Sierra Mountains. Gail Brevard and her partners are called in to investigate the case, and she decides she must go undercover in order to get to the truth of the matter. A cruel arson murder followed by an explosion at an old mine threaten Gail's life, as she and her colleague try to put all the pieces of the puzzle together and prevent further tragedy . . .

TERROR STRIKES

Norman Firth

To Chief Inspector Sharkey, the first murder is baffling enough: on a night-club dance floor, a man suddenly begins to choke. Horrified onlookers watch as he collapses and dies. It is quickly established that he has been strangled by someone standing directly behind him. But witnesses all testify that there was no one near him to do it. When this death is followed by a whole string of similar murders, Sharkey begins to seriously wonder if Scotland Yard is up against something supernatural . . .

THE JOCKEY

Gerald Verner

A man calling himself the Jockey begins a campaign against those who he believes have besmirched the good name of horse racing, escaping conviction through lack of evidence. In a message to the press, he vows that those who have amassed crooked fortunes will have the money taken from them, whilst those who have caused loss of life will find their own lives forfeit ... When the murders begin, Superintendent Budd of Scotland Yard is charged to find and stop the mysterious avenger. But is the Jockey the actual murderer?